CRACK-UP

Also by March Hastings

Abnormal Wife
Again and Again
The Boys of Brigham Dee
By Flesh Alone
Crack-Up
The Demands of the Flesh
Design for Debauchery
Enraptured
Fear of Incest
The Heat of the Day
Her Private Hell
The Jealous and Free
Obsessed
The Outcasts
A Rage Within
Savage Surrender
The Soft Way
Three Women
The Third Sex
The Third Theme
The Unashamed
Veil of Torment
Whip of Desire

CRACK-UP

MARCH HASTINGS

CUTTING EDGE

ISBN-13: 978-1-952138-84-3

Published by
Cutting Edge Books
PO Box 8212
Calabasas, CA 91372
www.cuttingedgebooks.com

CHAPTER ONE

A T THE SOUND of his footsteps, she arranged a smile across her features and turned to greet him.

She saw that his trained glance had found her trembling hands. Found them, then looked away again, kindly. He set the black instrument bag on the rug and came toward her. "Still worrying?" he said softly.

A pang of guilt singed her nerves. She leaned back against the windowsill and felt the cool drizzle blow in across her arms. "Yes, I suppose so." She tried to laugh. Tried to make it sound normal, her worry.

He stepped in close to her. "Karen, look at me."

His tone of command made her shudder. She didn't want to look at him, couldn't look him right in the eyes, She didn't dare. For he would see straight down to where the miserable need that would not die stirred even now.

His hands gripped her shoulders. "Be sensible, Karen. I've told you a dozen times that these checkups are only routine. There's no more danger." The hands shook her gently. "Do you hear me? No more danger."

She caught a deep breath and hung onto it as though for life. She could feel the heat of his palms through the thin material of her dress. *No more danger.* She didn't know whether to laugh or to cry. He was a doctor. Didn't he see? Didn't he suspect the new horror that had come into her life since Steve's accident?

"He'll be up and racing again before the year's out," he said in a calmer voice. "I promise you that."

She let the breath out slowly, trying to calm herself. "Thank you, Bill," she murmured. The words were barely audible.

"Don't thank me. Thank that physique of his."

She pulled away from him now, so he could not see her face. But what could she say? She couldn't tell him. She hardly dared admit it to herself, the truth about Steve's physique since the smash up. Yet this truth was making a monster out of her. Filling her nights with insane images and her days with moments like this. Moments that made her battle against the senseless urge to fling her body against Bill's and press, simply because he was a man.

She forced herself to turn away from him and stare out the window. The blur of city rooftops in the rain made a gray pattern against a steel gray sky. She had always loved this kind of Spring weather. A background for dreaming. Yet now there was only the background. The dreams, the hopes no longer belonged.

She felt Bill close behind her. "If you don't get hold of yourself," his voice came over her shoulder, "I'll have two patients here instead of one."

Wordlessly, she nodded. Why didn't he go? Why didn't he just retreat discreetly and leave her alone? What kind of a doctor was he that he didn't sense the real core of her trouble?

She felt his hand again. This time on her arm. Skin touching skin. She wanted desperately to lean back against him, to feel all of him pressing against her. Yet she knew he didn't mean anything. He couldn't possibly mean anything. And she stiffened, holding her body rigidly away from him.

There was a long moment of silence. She could feel his young face sink deeper into the craggy lines of thoughtfulness.

"Karen?"

She clung to the edge of the windowsill, her nails digging into the wood.

"Come sit down with me for a minute."

"It's nothing, Bill. Really," she lied. But she knew it was too late. She had given herself away this time. Her need had grown so large that it had pushed off the lid of superficial control. Yet she didn't dare put it into words. As long as it only happened inside her own head, she could pretend that it was nothing more important than a foolish anxiety.

But maybe she could still bluff him. Maybe. "All right, Dr. Stacy," her voice lilted artificially. She gestured behind them at the huge living room, the oversized sofa and deep pile carpeting giving off a sense of easy comfort. "Where would you like to hold this consultation?"

"Well, why don't we ..."

His voice was cut off abruptly by the distant tinkling of a bell.

Her body surged with relief. "Steve wants me," she said unnecessarily. She knew if she could just get away from Bill for a few seconds, she could somehow regain control of her senses.

He shrugged easily. "Go ahead," he said.

Hurriedly Karen swept past Bill and down the foyer. The energy of her desire translated into the sturdy bounce of her walk. The prospect of facing Steve confronted her like a reckoning with her own conscience. At the threshhold to his bedroom, she paused and smoothed her hands slowly along the ribline of her dress, cupping her breasts till the beating of her heart steadied. Then she lifted her chin and sailed graciously into the room.

"I didn't hear you close the door behind him," Steve said.

The barrel-deep voice she remembered came from him now with breathy discomfort. What had once been sunburn had become the yellow complexion of indoors and suffering. Their wedding picture stood on the dresser, looking out at them with the faces of two strangers. Happy strangers. Hard to believe that picture was only four months old.

"You didn't hear the door because he's still in the living room," she said cheerily.

She tucked the blankets a little neater around his waist and kissed him on the side of the nose. They were unnecessary motions, motions to make her seem busy. To convey to him that she was the happy little wife, his darling, all sunshine and loyalty.

"Oh?" he croaked.

She heard the suspicion in his voice and knew that it covered fear.

"Yes," she said lightly, sitting down on the edge of the mattress and resting her hand on his arm. "And he's promised me you'll be up and racing again in no time."

"Yeah."

"Steve, he wouldn't say it if he didn't mean it. Why should he?"

"Bedside manners."

"Darling, you're being foolish."

"Sure, foolish. Believe me, I feel pretty damned foolish lyin' here like a flat tire. Having to listen to his drivel."

"Let's not discuss it now," she said. "He might hear you."

Steve jerked his head away from under her lips. "What the hell do I care what he hears? Is he lyin' here like a goddamn ass?"

Karen ran her fingers along the edge of his crew cut. It was growing in a little and felt soft instead of bristly. "You mustn't upset yourself," she said. She had meant to be gentle, but the words sounded like chips of ice. And she knew that the constant nagging of her body was fast consuming the patience she needed for Steve.

His voice cut at her like a lash. "I'll get as upset as I damn please. Who's gonna stop me?"

She clamped her jaws shut, not wanting to contribute to the pattern of argument already becoming much too familiar. "If you want to lie here and eat yourself up alive, that's your privilege," she said. "But I want no part of it." She got off the bed in a quick motion and smoothed back whisps of hair from her temple. "I'm going to see Bill to the door before he hears what a fool you're making of yourself."

Without waiting for a reply, she left the room, anger and irritation bringing heat to her cheeks.

When she reached the living room, Bill was tearing a page off his prescription pad. He folded it and placed it on the ebony table in front of the couch.

"You fill that," he said, "and take one every night before retiring. It ought to do the trick."

Without realizing it, Karen breathed a deep sigh of relief. Steve had at least managed to divert attention away from herself, at least for the moment.

"But I hope," Bill's voice went on, "that you'll drop by my office one of these days. A routine check wouldn't do you any harm."

She heard the deep concern in his tone. Yet, before she could respond, he had turned and gone to pick up his bag. She knew there was really nothing more to say. And still, there was everything. She wanted to apologize, for Steve and for herself. But what were the words to tell Bill of her gratitude?

They reached the door together and he put his hand on the knob. "You let him complain all he wants," Bill said. "I know it's hard on you, but just remember it's worse for him. These active types have to let off steam somehow when they're confined. I'd really begin to worry if he were docile."

"Thank you, Bill," she said softly.

He winked at her and grinned. "See you kids Friday."

Then he was gone. Karen turned back slowly to face the large, silent apartment and Steve's grumpiness. With a sigh, she went out to the kitchen and busied herself fixing an um of coffee and some sandwiches for Steve's co-driver and pit man, expected at seven. She had gotten as far as buttering half a dozen slices of bread when the bell tinkled again. She closed her eyes and bit down hard on her lip. She didn't want to fight with him. She didn't want to hear the cranky voice that made a child out of what had once been her man.

And yet she had to go to him. For all the arguing and the pettiness, he needed to know that she was there … if only to take whatever nastiness he had to dish out.

She rinsed her hands and dried them slowly, observing how the pearl-pink nail polish glimmered in delicate ovals. She had promised herself always to remain attractive for him. Regardless. It wasn't necessarily a permanent thing with him, after all. He stood every chance in the world of recovering his masculinity along with his ability to walk. She knew that. All she had to do was hang onto her control. And pray.

"What took you so long this time?" he said.

"If all you want to do is fight with me, Steve, I'm not going to stay in this room with you. I'm in the middle of fixing a snack for Allen and Spots."

"Has Bill gone?"

"Yes."

"Do you s'pose he heard me?"

She gazed at the gray eyes, limpid now as melting steel, and her heart seemed to grow large inside her chest with aching. "Oh, Steve … Steve." She put her face into the collar of his pajamas. "I love you so much."

She stretched out on the bed, trying not to snuggle too tightly against him. Yet her breasts, seemingly with a will of their own, pressed against his arm, their nipples hardening, yearning toward the memory of his kisses.

"Honey, take it easy." A self-conscious laugh underlined his words.

Instantly her body stiffened. "I'm sorry," she said quickly, moving away. "I didn't mean to make you uncomfortable."

"You just gotta take it easy for a while." His voice was low, wary.

"I know it, darling," she murmured. "I don't understand what gets into me sometimes. I only wanted to hold you, that's all." Her languid tone seemed to wind around him. "Only hold you, Steve."

"Sure, I know," he said. "It's plenty hard on you. On me, too, you know. I mean, you're not all alone in the way you feel."

A dizzying twinge began in the pit of her stomach and reached downward. Suddenly she needed him desperately with an urgency that would not wait. She pressed against him, caressing his jaw with her fingertips.

"You want to touch me, don't you, darling?" she whispered. "You want to hold me." Her lips were moist. "There's nobody in the world I want the way I want you. Want to kiss you … love you …"

"Karen, baby, sure I want you. Only not now," he rasped. "Not now, I said."

His harshness whipped her back to reality. Her gaze came back into focus and she saw the tight, strained look around his mouth. The look that meant all his words were lies. That he didn't feel a thing anymore. Not a flicker. That there was nothing for her but the emptiness she saw reflected in the dullness of his eyes.

It might last a week. It might last two weeks. Or it might last forever. She had no way of knowing what to expect from the future, beyond the strangling hand of desire around her own throat. And how could she learn to live with it? After only three months of fulfillment, how could she be expected to resign herself to the desert of abstinence?

And yet she loved him as she loved life itself.

"Would you like me to bring you some coffee?" she said, her voice shaking.

"Yeah, that would be nice, honey." He tried to smile wickedly.

She did not even notice the smile. She was aware only of the relief in his voice, the genuine gladness.

Why doesn't he tell me? she thought. *Why doesn't he tell me it's all over with? Maybe, if he would only say something, I could*

7

learn to get used to it. Anything but this God-awful masquerade. Why dosen't he say it?

In a quick, nervous motion, she got up off the bed and stepped into her shoes. There was no reason, after all, to flaunt her need in front of him. It only served to make them both uncomfortable.

Yet, inside its clothing, her body felt desolate. Somehow her thighs, her hips, her breasts didn't connect up with her brain. Didn't hear the signals that said there was no use trying. That Steve no longer desired her and there was no point in forcing her attentions on him. She was beginning to feel like two women in one being. The loving, faithful wife and the screaming, wild harlot.

She dug her nails deep into her palms and tried to draw blood.

CHAPTER TWO

WHEN SHE WAS alone once more in the kitchen, Karen leaned against the refrigerator and closed her eyes. Her tongue felt dry and swollen. Inside her chest, a crazy throbbing had started. The sensations were familiar ones, recalling those first few moments after Steve's car had turned over. And she knew they were the sensations of dread.

Dimly Karen realized that she must fight against the panic growing inside her. She pulled the stepladder out of the broom closet and took a bottle of apricot brandy down from the high cupboard. The stuff would brace her. Steady her nerves. She poured some into a water glass and swallowed it quickly. The burning and the warmth helped. She shivered once, then drank some cold water to clear away the heat from her mouth. Already she felt better. Much better.

Still, her reflection in the chromium toaster showed a small, pale, drawn face. Hardly what Steve's friends would consider the appearance of an adequate wife. Leaving the half-finished sandwiches, she went to the bathroom and applied eye-shadow, mascara and rouge to make up for her own growing pallor. She fastened a string of crystals around her neck to add a final touch of shifting rainbow colors.

The heaviness in her arms seemed to lift. And, as she went back to the kitchen, she was humming almost cheerfully.

Promptly at seven, the doorbell rang.

There was something uncannily exact about Steve's racing friends that had always unnerved her. She supposed it had to do with the nature of their profession, this almost compulsive precision. Yet it set her on edge. She felt that they judged and measured her, that they had all her weaknesses neatly catalogued. And now was certainly no time for her to be transparent.

She took a deep breath to steady herself as she swung open the door. There were only two, Allen and his blonde wife Jean. Two eager faces, waiting for her to cope with them.

"Hello, Karen." Jean kissed her lightly below the earlobe and Karen smelled the faint aroma of heather, felt the touch of cool lips.

"Hi, honey," Allen said, smiling his broad, chubby smile. The flowered sports shirt beneath his raincoat looked cleaner than anything she had ever seen on him before.

Clean enough for a funeral, Karen thought. And for an instant she felt a rush of uncertainty. Allen and Jean were the first visitors Steve had been allowed. She prayed that they might not upset him.

The blurred chatter of their voices buzzed around her while she led them into the living room and went to fix drinks.

Allen launched into the sandwiches and Jean arranged her long, slim body on the couch.

"I thought Spots and Annette would be with you," Karen said casually as she handed Jean a glass.

"Um hmm," Jean smiled. "So did we. But they're having troubles and…" She finished the sentence with a wave of her hand. Her emerald green eyes glittered for a moment with an amusement Karen did not understand.

"Don't listen to Jean," Allen mumbled around a bite of sandwich. "She's always making a big deal out of nothing."

Karen glanced from one to the other of them curiously. They seemed an odd couple, not at all suited to each other. Allen, rough-hewn, clumsy, balding. And Jean, cool, sophisticated, aloof. It bothered her vaguely to hear Jean commenting on the private lives of other people. She seemed somehow immune to gossip. And Karen sensed that there must be something special in this particular bit of news.

Still, she did not wish to probe. She said quietly, "Steve's awake and anxious to see you."

Allen nodded stiffly and she realized that her words had dropped into a bed of fear. It was as though he had come to pay his last respects rather than just to visit. And, although she knew it was simply because every race driver was constantly plagued by the phantom of death, her throat tightened with anger. She wanted suddenly to claw at his face, to scream at him to smile. She wanted to shout at him that Steve was all right. That Bill Stacy had said so.

"Well, come along then." She spoke as easily as she could over the tight ball of fury knotted in her chest.

When they entered the bedroom, she saw Steve sitting propped up on the pillows, expectantly.

A glimmer of life returned to his eyes as he greeted his friend.

"Hi, there, ol' buddy," he said hoarsely. He nudged Allen for a cigarette.

Allen dropped the pack on the night table beside the bed. Then he drew up a chair and lit a cigarette for each of them.

It wasn't five minutes before the conversation had turned to Ferraris and the latest speedsters out of Mercedes Benz.

Karen felt much too nervous to listen to shop talk. She stood still for a few minutes, fidgeting inwardly, waiting for a chance to interrupt. Finally she blurted, "If you'll excuse me, I'll bring the drinks in here."

She saw Steve nod absently, then push her even further from his interest with an impatient gesture of his fingers. Karen sighed and started for the door.

"I'll give you a hand," Jean said with an amused tone. "This tech talk has me up to here." She moved a pointed fingernail across her throat. "They'll never notice we're gone anyway."

Karen nodded and managed a cheerful smile. "They're demons," she said. "Not men."

They moved along the foyer now. She sensed Jean's body beside, yet slightly behind her. It seemed to give off a protecting warmth that made Karen want to talk, to confide some of the feelings pressing tensely against her insides. Yet she hardly knew the woman at all.

"All dedicated people are demons," Jean said, her tone low and casual. In the living room she paused to light a cigarette and Karen noticed the long curve of her thighs outlined by the tight linen skirt.

Jean dropped the match into a crystal ash tray. "You don't smoke," she said with authority.

"How did you know?"

Jean shrugged. "I'm the observant type."

"Well, maybe I ought to learn," Karen said with sudden vehemence. "I seem to be all out of step with everything." Her hands trembled with the violence of her emotion.

Calmly, Jean picked up the bourbon bottle and poured them each a drink. "It's pretty rough playing nursemaid, isn't it?" She came over to Karen and put a glass into her hand. "It would get anybody down. That's why I've made Allen promise to quit when he's got enough money saved to buy into a decent business."

Karen shook her head slowly. "I don't think I could ever talk Steve into that. I know he'll be racing again the minute he's able to. That's all he thinks about." She swallowed some of the whiskey and savored the bitter taste on her tongue. "But I'll never understand it. I mean, these people are grown men. How can they get such a thrill out of…"

"Don't try to understand it," Jean interrupted. Her heavy eyelids lowered slightly, casting shadows over her eyes in the growing dusk. "People get thrills out of many things."

"It's all too confusing," Karen said, feeling the bitterness in her mouth spread through her body. "If I could only see an end to it, a solution."

Jean sat down in the reading chair and stretched her tanned legs out in front of her, crossing them at their slim ankles. "You ought to break it up a little." She gazed at the ice cubes in her glass. "I mean, find some other interests before you get addicted to the worry." She hesitated, then finished her drink in a quick movement.

"I appreciate the advice, Jean. But ... Well, you don't just start to take singing lessons."

Jean sat up and her wide forehead wrinkled with concern. "I didn't mean it to sound so cruel," she said quietly. "But I guess it does boil down to that in the long run. Cruelty. For the time being, though, I'd rather we called it self-preservation. *Your* preservation, Karen."

She emphasized the word with a strange sincerity that left Karen unable to reply.

"I know what you're thinking," Jean continued, lighting a second cigarette from the first. "Or rather, feeling. You're feeling guilty to be talking about you instead of what's happened to Steve. You're feeling that it isn't right, somehow, to be sick and tired of all this anxiety."

"I don't want to discuss it," Karen blurted. Embarrassment echoed in her strained voice. She felt as though her forehead were made out of glass and that Jean was reading the words of her conscience written out there.

"Of course not," Jean said in the quiet tone that left no room for argument. "That's why I was doing the talking...so you wouldn't have to."

Karen swallowed hard and forced herself to search the woman's face. She had never known friendship like this. Nor had she ever needed it before. Steve had filled her life completely.

Satisfyingly. He filled it now. Yet the worry and the fear and the loneliness were real companions that she dared not deny. And here was a human voice, a human spirit who shared almost the same concerns. Could she accept this friendship? Dare she allow anything to divert her attention from Steve, even for an instant?

"That's right, honey," Jean's voice interrupted her thoughts. "Look me over. Look to see what kind of person would talk to you like this right in your own home." Her wide lips gave a subtle animation to her mouth.

"Why?" Karen faltered. "Why are you saying all this to me, Jean?"

Jean's shoulders drooped for a moment as though she were recalling a sad memory. "Who knows?"

An impulse to reach out and touch Jean's hand, to comfort in turn this woman who had comforted her had collided now with her duty to get back into the bedroom with the refreshments. The alcohol and the brandy were not mixing well in her brain. Fuzziness where there had once been clarity confused her desires. Strangely, she felt that she was not really wanted there. That certainly, she was not being missed. She imagined Steve, engrossed in his man's world. Recalling past days of grease-stained glory. Making plans, perhaps futile ones, for other days to come. Reliving for a few precious hours his shattered masculinity. It was all so useless, so senseless, so utterly beyond her.

She carried her empty glass toward the bottle.

"That's not the way," Jean said. "You don't drown anything unless you drown yourself." She laughed quickly then at her words. "In case you hadn't noticed, this is wisdom Thursday. You can tune in on me every Tuesday, Thursday and Saturday. Same time. Same station."

Unaccountably, Karen felt herself relaxing. "Come on," she said. "I'll fill your glass, too."

They sat for a while, sipping their drinks without talking, watching together the night lights flick on across the city. A fragrant breath of fresh, green air blew in from Central Park, touching Karen's nostrils, reminding her that there was still another world outside. She had remained indoors for almost a month, calling down for groceries and medication, sleeping at odd hours of the day or night. Hearing only Steve's voice, Steve's requests for comforts.

"I have been narrow-minded," she said, half to Jean, half to herself. "My own demon of dedication." She smiled wryly. "But one that didn't work out so well."

It helped a little to put the thought into words, relieved a little of the fear. And she felt the stirring of hope for the first time in many days. For it was possible that a change of scene, a change of pace might be all that she needed to check the outrage of desire which burned so irreverantly. It was only natural that her attention should have focused on sex when there was nothing to divert her mind or body from the suppression required.

Yes, the more she considered it, the more hopeful she became.

She stood up suddenly and switched on a table lamp, no longer afraid to face herself and her feelings. She moved easily to the decanter and poured fresh drinks to take into the bedroom. Yet she knew it was only duty that drew her back. She was sick to death of the smell of medicine and illness.

She turned to find the emerald dark eyes of her new found friend examining her and smiled reassuringly. "Thanks," she said simply. "You've helped."

"Anytime," Jean said. She took the tray from Karen and started out to the foyer.

Even as she walked toward the bedroom that was no longer her bedroom, really, Karen felt the surge of confidence beginning to wane. After all, what substitute would she be able to find, what substitute could there be for the loss of a husband's embrace?

She felt old suddenly and tired. Her legs began to ache with a sense of futility. Narrow paths of pain shot up to the small of her back and vibrated there. She hardly listened to the drone of conversation, her thoughts, her fears consuming her attention.

What if she did begin to see more of Jean…more of other people in general? Where would it lead her? What would she find?

By the time Jean and Allen had gone, Karen was thoroughly depressed. She went out to the kitchen and began slowly to clean up the dishes. But very slowly. For she knew she was drunk.

She had certainly not intended to lose control of herself. It had crept up on her sneakily. The black and white squares of linoleum began to sway a little. Like rumba hips. In her head she began to hear the slow music to go with the moving floor. She held out her arms to an imaginary partner and began to dance. She felt her breasts swelling inside the bra cups. The nipples hardening, pressing against the material almost painfully. She blinked a few times and hummed the tune hoarsely. She leaned her cheek against an imaginary chest and closed her eyes.

Dizziness overwhelmed her. She swallowed hard and spread her legs to keep her balance. Abruptly she stopped the foolish game and forced her eyes open. Perspiration streamed down the sides of her arms, staining the delicate material of her dress. Unhooking it down the back, she let it fall to the floor and stepped clear. The rayon slip clung to her buttocks like massaging palms.

She reached the sink but could not wash the dishes. Turning on the cold water, she spattered her forehead and cheeks. The pussy cat clock ticked loudly above the kitchenette table. She clung to the edge of the sink and listened to the rhythmic sound, feeling as though there were someone in the room with her, watching and condemning her. But there was no one, nothing except the seven sprawling rooms gathering dust in the darkness.

And Steve, restlessly asleep beneath the woolen blanket. Dreaming of racetracks. Her Steve. Her darling, shattered inside this hulk of a man fast growing to be a stranger.

Turning to the clock, she squinted up at its idiot grin and saw the time. Only eleven. She knew she would not fall asleep until two or three. What would she do with herself until then?

The dishes. Finish the dishes. Then scrub the floor. Maybe polish all the silver again.

In the sudsy water, a cup slipped out of her fingers and gurgled down to the bottom of the pan. How do you get sober?

Tomato juice?

The cupboard showed no tomato, but a large can of vegetable juice that would have to do.

Hardly had she gulped the stuff down when she felt it rising from her rebellious stomach. Just time enough to dash to the bathroom and kneel before the bowl.

Panting and clammy, she relaxed beside it, promising herself that it would never do for her to get drunk again. *You don't drown anything unless you drown yourself.* Jean had been right. But how does one learn to be debonaire?

Suddenly she saw vividly the image of herself, sitting on the cold bathroom tile, the slip wrinkled up above her knees, her stockings twisted. She smiled wryly. Debonaire, indeed. She had to start learning all over again how to be decent.

Tiredly Karen dragged herself back onto her feet and turned on an ice cold shower. She pulled off her slip, slid out of her garterbelt and panties. She opened her bra and the heavy breasts sagged undesired. She cupped and lifted them in her palms. The merest touch, even of her own hands, seemed to whip them to fire.

Blindly she stepped into the streaming spray and bit her lip hard as her body began to shiver.

When she finally came out onto the bathmat, every nerve in her body felt flayed to death. She patted herself dry and sprinkled powder into the damp crevices.

The sound of Steve's bell alerted her attention.

"I'll be right with you," she called. There was no robe for her to put on, no decent clothing. She fastened a towel around her in sarong fashion and tucked the end in tightly between her breasts. Then she padded quickly out to him.

The tiny night light beside his bed suffused the room with a soft pink glow.

"Thirsty," he mumbled.

She poured ice water from the thermos and leaned over to lift him enough to drink.

Holding the glass with his big hand over hers, he took a few swallows, then pushed it away. But he continued to hold onto her.

"What's this get up?" he said.

"I just took a bath, Steve, that's all."

He pulled her closer, his strong fingers twined now around her wrist. "You smell pretty strange for someone who's just taken a bath."

"Must be the powder."

"No. Not powder."

She wanted to back away from him but he clung to her wrist. "I don't know what you mean unless it's the whiskey on my breath."

He shook his head. "Not that either."

"Well, then, I can't imagine ..."

"I know what it is, damn you."

He wrenched away from her now. She could see the muscle in his jaw flexing with anger.

"Steve, please. What is it?"

"You know damn well what it is."

"No, Steve. I don't."

"Lying bitch ... whore ..."

The words lashed out and she moved away from them. There was no answer to give, no excuse, no denial. Somehow he had managed to discover her difficulty. Only by calling her names could he divert the blame away from himself. She knew she dare not attack or accuse him in return. She stood quite still, waiting for his anger to spend itself.

"So this is how you promise to love, honor and obey." His voice was cold, deliberately cruel.

"I do love you, Steve."

"Filthy minded ..." He sighed with pain at his own exertion. "Gutter tramp."

"I love you, Steve."

"Prancing around the house naked, drunk."

"I love you, Steve."

"Thinking of ... who the hell knows what."

His eyes seemed to bulge with a disgust and hatred she had never seen in him before. That she had never dreamed he might feel for her.

Yet his disgust was no greater than her own, she had to admit.

Turning away from his distorted features, unable to bear the accusation in his eyes, she took a nightgown from the chest of drawers and slipped it on over her head. That it had become necessary to hide her body from him made of their marriage an ugly farce.

She left him as soon as she could and ran to bury her face in the cushions of the divan, letting the hot tears overwhelm her.

CHAPTER THREE

B Y MORNING, KAREN knew she would have to see Bill Stacy, admit everything to him, and ask for professional help.

She and Bill had been friends since high school days. He had always been someone to depend on. And that was certainly what she needed now. Yet, even as she made the decision to speak to him, she hesitated. Her problem was such an intimate one. She could not even broach the subject to her own husband. How would she approach it with another man?

Carefully she picked out her most sedate cotton dress and buckled on the wide belt, hoping that the loose folds hid the curves of her body and might thereby negate the lustfulness of her conversation.

As she moved around the bedroom, she occasionally glimpsed Steve's reflection in one of the mirrors. This would be the first time that she had left him alone since the accident. And she knew that he was watching her closely, suspiciously.

Finally, she turned to face him squarely. There was nothing to hide, after all, and she wanted him to know her every move if it would make him rest easier. "I'm going to Bill's office," she said bluntly. "I think I may need a sedative to get me to sleep nights."

As she spoke, Karen remembered the neglected prescription on the living room table. Really, all she had to do was send for it to be filled. But she continued combing the short bangs across her forehead. She saw the thin line of Steve's lips and knew that he didn't believe her. Yet he said nothing. He only sighed a deep breath of disgust and pulled the blanket tighter around his chest.

"I won't be gone an hour," she went on. "You won't have to take any pills until I get back." She spoke mechanically, efficiently, poised tensely for another verbal attack.

He turned his head away and closed his eyes.

"Have you taken a vow of silence?" She spoke casually, trying to be debonaire in the way she imagined someone like Jean would be.

He reached a glass of orange juice off the serving tray she'd prepared and sipped at it.

"Steve, stop being childish," she snapped, letting some of the impatience creep into her tone.

He sighed again, replaced the glass and snuggled down as though for a nap.

"All right," she said more gently. "Have it your way. Make life as difficult as possible for both of us."

Though she managed to maintain a surface calm, Karen felt a nervous throbbing begin in either temple. Quickly she checked the contents of her purse, smoothed on a pair of white cotton gloves and fled Steve's presence. The subtle aroma of her own Rose cologne cloyed at her nostrils. Her arms, her legs, her total being seemed too much to bear.

Outside, a weak sun rode high behind close-knit clouds and the air felt chill with dampness. She had always loved to walk in this weather and memories of younger, freer days mingled vaguely with the more distinct image of her destination. The noises of traffic, the jostling of people excited her, firing her with energy and a desire to see and do all the things she had been missing since Steve's confinement. Now that she was out of the house for a little while, life didn't seem so grim after all. And as she approached the door to Bill's office, she was no longer sure of what she had wanted to say to him.

Yet she had told Steve that she was coming here. She knew that, considering the frame of mind he was in, she'd better not give him the chance to call her a liar.

In the waiting room she opened a magazine and glanced at it from time to time. The brown leather chairs all looked well sat in, the pile of magazines neatly arranged, the receptionist busy with typing. Bill's practice was obviously successful, the reward for diligence and sincerity.

"Why didn't you phone?" he scolded as she entered the office. "You know I'd have come in for you." He took her hands and held them between his own, as one holds a child taking its first steps.

"I needed these few minutes to pull my thoughts together," she replied truthfully.

"Tell me about it." He sat down on the edge of his desk, pushing a couple of medical journals aside.

"Aren't you going to lean back in your swivel chair?" She said it jokingly, but beneath the banter, she knew she would feel more comfortable with the desk between them. This way, he could look deep into her eyes, down to the very center of her trouble. And she did not want him to see more than she was prepared to show.

"All right, I'll sit in the swivel chair." He swung off the desk and leaned back in the large, wide chair, resting his elbows on the arms and crossing his fingers beneath his chin. "Better?"

"Don't laugh at me, Bill."

"I'm not. I'm only trying to please you."

"That seems to be rather difficult."

"What does?"

"Pleasing me," she said simply. "I don't seem to be getting along with anyone. Especially Steve."

Behind Bill, the door to the examination room stood ajar. Her glance wandered past his shoulder, to the long table covered with the white paper that crinkled so when one sat on it. She knew she had to tell Bill everything. She wanted to, after all. Yet she couldn't possibly do it if she looked him straight in the eyes.

"We both know that Steve isn't the easiest patient in the world," Bill said. "But this is certainly no cause for alarm. You've stood up to him like a veteran. And when he's back on his feet again, he'll be proud of you for it. Right now, we don't expect Steve to be anything more than a cranky child."

A single bead of perspiration slid down her left side. She felt it and shivered. "There's more to it than Steve's crankiness."

"More to what, dear?"

She heard the professional tone click on in Bill's voice and knew it could only mean that she had conveyed part of her anxiety.

"Would I be here about something you've told me a thousand times already?"

"Possibly." He began to move his chair back and forth in a small arc.

Slowly, she pulled off her gloves, finger by finger. "But not probably." Now she forced herself to look at him. Her eyelids burned from lack of sleep, the tendons in her neck seemed to be straining outward. She wanted Bill to see this, to see the ravages her nerves had wrought on her body. Surely these were not the symptoms of a person who was basically happy.

Bill remained silent, his eyes watching her narrowly.

"Well, aren't you going to help me?" she said plaintively.

"In every way I can."

But he couldn't say it for her. She knew that. Nor could she expect him to understand if she would not say it for herself.

"Well, it is about Steve and me," she began, pressing her nails into the soft leather of her purse. "We ... We haven't been getting along. At all. Not at all." She faltered. The room seemed unbearably quiet. "In fact, we've been arguing lately. Not just cranky arguments, as you've suggested. But bitterly."

The pattern of sunshine on the floor in the other room was beginning to lengthen. The curtains fluttered a little. She wished she could leap up and run out of here before she had to say any more. Yet she knew there must be no running away from her problem, no false modesty, no misplaced demureness.

"Go on," Bill encouraged. He had stopped rocking the chair and took an oilskin pouch from the desk drawer. He began to fill his pipe, using the same careful movements with which he approached everything.

Karen cleared her throat but the lump which seemed to be lodged behind her tongue did not go away. "Of course I didn't expect there to be any love in our lives. Romantic love, I mean. I'm not a monster, Bill. At least, I don't think I am." She looked at him questioningly.

"Of course you aren't," he said positively.

She shook her head. "Yet it turns out that I am. I really am." Her voice broke and she had to press her lips together to maintain her composure.

"I understand you." He spoke around the pipe stem, moving the flame of his lighter in slow circles. "You're a young woman. A healthy young woman, I might add. You talk about this as though you don't realize I know everything you mean to say. As Steve's doctor, I think you might give me a little more credit." His eyes smiled as he spoke.

"I don't know what to do," she said flatly. "It's driving me out of my mind."

"Do you mean your sexual desire or Steve's impotence?"

Karen stared at him wordlessly.

"Don't look so shocked," he said mildly. "Just answer the question."

"Well…" She pressed her back against the chair to hold herself steady. "I didn't think there was a difference."

"But there is. A great one."

"How?"

He leaned forward and rested one elbow on the desk top. "One can be cured, the other endured. And I don't mean it to sound like a maxim from seventh grade hygiene."

Karen's glance dropped to the neat, tight knot of his tie. "Is it a permanent thing, then?" She felt deflated. Dry. Tired.

"It's a possibility. But many men can't, you know."

"No, I didn't know," she said vehemently.

"But you do know that you need ... diversion."

She frowned impatiently. "Bill, after all these years of friendship, why are you speaking to me like a lecherous old man?"

"I'm afraid that's your distortion," he said quietly. "You're over-anxious, which I understand. You need release, which I also understand. And," his body inclined toward her almost imperceptibly, "you must know how much I've cared for you all these years."

"Yes, yes." She was beginning to feel annoyed, even a little afraid. Not quite sure what he was getting at and not at all sure she wanted to find out. "We've been very good friends, Bill. In my own way I love you. I always have."

"But not the way you love Steve Edgemont." His calm eyes remained level, yet there was the barest tinge of bitterness in his voice.

"Bill, he's my husband." She sounded a little desperate even to herself. She saw his eyes begin to probe her.

He touched his fingertips together thoughtfully. "After a fashion," he said finally. "I wonder if you ever really considered just why you married him? How long did you know the man before the two of you ran off? Three weeks? Or was it six?" He pressed his lips together. "It doesn't really matter. But I stood by and watched it happen. And I think I understand. You didn't want love and a home with him. You weren't interested in raising a family. What you wanted, Karen, was thrills. The uncertain life of chasing from city to city. Never truly knowing what lay in store for you from one day to the next."

"But ..." she sputtered.

"No, don't try to interrupt me. I've known you too long, too well and from too many angles. Look at you. Now that the thrills are gone, you're frightened because you feel trapped. You can't face the thought of spending the rest of your life with a sexually incompetent man. Even if you do profess to love him. No, you can't imagine it. And frankly, I don't blame you."

He pushed himself out of the chair and came toward her.

"What are you telling me?" She spoke in a voice hardly audible. A series of shivers chased along the insides of her arms. She knew what was coming, knew she should break away and run from him. Yet she remained immobile, watching warily as he approached.

"I'm telling you to live a little, my friend. To forget all the rules you've learned about morals. When you see sickness and death every day, as I do, you begin to understand what a farce our petty morality is. One suffers enough involuntarily. Why add to the burden?"

"I've never heard you speak like this before, Bill."

"Perhaps not."

He took her by the arms and lifted her up from the chair. She felt numb and limp as though the blood had been drained from her veins. In her head she heard the echo of what he had said about Steve. Permanent impotence. No hope, really.

"But how do you know he won't get better?" she pleaded. "How do you know for sure?"

"I don't know for sure. Maybe, in five years. With therapy. One ever knows anything for sure. But are you willing to wait around to find out?"

She paused, then raised her chin defiantly. "Yes, I am," she said with all the determination she could muster.

He shook his head slowly. "That's not true, Karen. You might as well admit it."

He held her tightly by both forearms and pulled her to him. She felt his mouth stingingly on hers. A dizziness whirled behind her forehead. His hands slid along her spine down to the small of her back and pressed her hips to his.

She knew she ought to kick, to scream. But she remembered Steve. The names he had called her. And now she knew the same desperation he must have known. A desperation that blinded her, filled her with craving. Demanded release.

She let herself go limp against him. He half dragged, half carried her into the examination room, pushing the door shut with his heel. She heard the crisp paper wrinkling beneath her. His hands moved the clothes off her body in quick, economical movements. She lifted her weight so he could pull down her panties.

For a while, as he undressed, she stared at the gray ceiling. Then his hands began searching out the tender areas of her flesh, trailing paths of flame along her belly, down to her thighs.

She closed her eyes. A low moan rolled deep in her throat. Her own hands moved to find him.

He pressed her thighs wide and she gasped on an intake of breath. The painful thrill of it swelled through her. Her body slid along the paper and she heard it tear. The heat of Bill's body urged her to give. Her limbs encircled him ... clung ... swayed.

"Make it happen," she whispered.

And then her insides seemed to shatter into a million sparking pieces of life.

His mouth mashed down on hers, drowning the shriek that had risen to her throat.

And then they were separate again.

She lay on the table, unable to move just yet, watching him dress, deliberately, slowly, neatly.

"How do you feel?" he said.

She could hardly speak. Her tongue felt thick and heavy with a misery she could not define. "Don't you dare use that clinical tone to me," she managed finally.

And she knew that she hated Bill. Hated him totally, with the completeness of her being and her desire.

Hated him, yet would return again and again to his eager arms.

CHAPTER FOUR

KAREN STUMBLED OUT into the glaring sunlight and stared around her, wide-eyed, surprised that the world was still there. Automatically she started toward home, but when she reached the corner, she found that she could not make herself cross the street.

Impossible, now, to face Steve.

Impossible, when Bill came to visit, to pretend that he was only the family doctor.

A whore and a tramp she might be, but she was a terrible liar. Yet, unless she wanted to walk out on Steve right now, she would have to lie. Both for his sake and for her own.

And the first lie would have to be to her mother.

She found a phone booth and dialled. Her mother agreed readily to stay with Steve for a few hours, glad that Karen had at long last decided to break up the routine.

And then she was back on the street again, free for the rest of the day.

Free with nowhere to go, unable to think of a soul she dared to face.

Her mind whirled with the things Bill had said to her. Was she a thrill kid? Had she married Steve for such childish, superficial reasons?

Wandering into Central Park, she strolled around the Zoo midst the laughter of children, feeling terribly alone, isolated somehow from the rest of the human race. And yet, she could not really agree with what Bill had said. She did want a home.

And children. Of course she did. How different if she could be here today with a child of Steve's instead of the guilt that seemed to be dragging at her skirts.

She climbed the few steps onto the terrace and went inside the cafeteria for a glass of iced tea. The clatter of silverware and dishes added to the throbbing in her head. She found a cool spot to sit down with her drink and tried again to regain control of her emotions.

The straws had gone soggy, the ice cubes melted and the remains of her lipstick nervously smeared onto a crinkled napkin before Karen felt steady enough to get up again.

She could not yet bring herself to go home to Steve, to face his suspicious, her mother's sharp intuition. What she needed more than anything was someone to talk to who would not try to probe.

Making her way between ice cream carts and baby carriages, she hailed a cab on Fifth Avenue and gave the driver Jean's address. Jean, at least, would not condemn her.

She had never been to Allen's home at the tip of the Bronx. And now, as she paid the fare and surveyed the rambling, shingle building, its dark green trimming harsh on the eyes, Karen wondered how Jean could possibly be happy here. She felt a vague sensation of repulsion, yet she hurriedly climbed the slanting wooden steps and rang the doorbell. She would have been thankful for company anywhere just now.

She listened to the harsh ring tear again through the house, trying at the same time to peer through the heavily curtained windows of the door. Finally she saw her friend's lithe body moving along the hall and she shuddered involuntarily with relief.

"Well, hi there," Jean said, taking off dark rimmed sun glasses. "I was just snoozing in the back yard." She wore a white polo shirt and blue denim shorts that fit almost as tightly as a bathing suit. Her skin glistened with suntan lotion and gave off its faintly sweet odor.

Karen stepped quickly inside as though she were sneaking into a hideout.

"Hey, what's with you?" Jean's laughter held the same bantering amusement Karen remembered.

"Running from the cops," Karen imitated her manner.

"I believe it."

The inside of the house belied its external appearance. Modern furniture, sparse but obviously comfortable, gave the rooms a tone of easy living. She followed Jean through the long hall and out into the backyard.

Another woman, also in shorts, reclined in a sun chair. Her taffy brown hair was pulled back tightly into a chignon, emphasizing the high cheek bones and making her look prematurely old.

"You know Annette?" Jean said.

"Certainly we know each other," Annette replied with a tight little smile that questioned Karen's presence.

Karen felt Jean's hand on her shoulder, moving her down onto another chair. She almost regretted having come here, now that Annette had made it all too clear that she was intruding on something private.

"Karen's hiding out, too," Jean said easily, taking up a pitcher of lemonade and pouring some into a tall, frosted glass. "Yes, I told Karen you and Spots were having trouble. You two have loads in common."

A hot flush of embarrassment suffused Karen's cheeks. But she took the glass quietly and stared over its rim at the rows of orange and violet flowers that bordered the well tended lawn. A tall wooden fence closed the yard off from its neighbors. Only muted sounds from the street, the occasional yelling of mother to child reminded her that this was still city living.

"Three blind mice," Annette said heavily. "See how they run."

Karen's glance darted quickly to Jean. Was she, too, involved with such matters?

"Oh, yes," Jean answered her silent question. "I claim no immunity." She stretched out in a wicker chair and tilted her face toward the sun. "This little back yard is a haven for wayward wives." She laughed. "And I don't even have to open my eyes to see the how-did-you-know expression on your delightful little face."

Karen felt the automatic impulse to deny it rise, then die inside her. She had needed to find someplace where she could be herself. Well, she had it. She kicked off her high heeled shoes and wiggled her toes.

"That's right," Annette said, watching her. "Relax until sundown. Then we all crawl back into our sheepskins for the night."

"You haven't crawled back into yours for two weeks," Jean said behind the flare of a match.

"So much the better for me." Annette leaned forward to reach the light.

A prickly hostility seemed to fill the air which Karen had neither expected nor understood. These women, instead of being the fast friends she had thought them to be, were actually attacking each other. Subtly, but viciously nevertheless. It didn't make much sense, but she had the impression that her sudden appearance on the scene had a lot to do with it.

"But we know all about us," Jean said, "and nothing about Karen." She looked at Karen and smiled ruefully. "So you took my advice and it exploded in your charming little hand, did it?"

"Yes, tell us," Annette added, exhaling smoke from her thin nostrils. "Tell us everything."

And now Karen was certain that her presence was an irritant, at least to Annette. But how could she retreat now without Jean thinking her utterly mad? Hadn't she made enough trouble for one day?

"Let the child rest," Jean put in soothingly. "She'll talk when she's ready. Or not at all, if that pleases her better."

Annette turned away angrily. And angrily she flicked an ash onto the grass and let it roll.

Jean ignored her. Calmly she folded her hands over her diaphragm and sat that way, looking at Karen.

Karen nodded thanks for being let alone. She felt an aura of protectiveness emanating toward her from Jean. An aura that soothed and offered the promise of forgetfulness. She had felt it last evening, but not so strongly then. Perhaps because she had not needed it so much.

In seemed doubly incomprehensible, therefore, that Annette should be so hostile.

"Well," Annette murmured. "I see times have changed." She swung her legs off the chair and searched out a pair of Mexican straw shoes.

"You're leaving us," Jean said blandly.

"Don't sound so anxious, doll. I do it every time."

Curiously Karen observed the interplay of emotions coiling out snakelike between the women. Obviously, they were old friends. And old friends reserved the right to quarrel, she told herself. Yet she did not enjoy being a witness to it. It seemed that her whole life was becoming a series of antagonisms, of petty destructive actions leading ultimately to turmoil.

"I wish there were something stronger in this drink than lemon juice," she said impulsively.

Both women turned to look at her.

"Give the girl a drink, Jean. You don't want to keep her thirsty." The voice was almost taunting.

"If you're going...go." Jean put her hand on the woman's behind and pushed gently.

"If the alcohol's coming out, I just might decide to stay," Annette purred.

"No whiskey." The words snapped with decision. "You know that, Annette."

"Poor little Karen." Annette waved one ringed hand at her. "No whiskey."

Karen sat quite still as Jean took the woman by the wrist and led her back to the house, half dragging, half cajoling. She wondered if Annette were going home now to Spots. If she herself would be going home later to Steve. And she almost wished that the sun would never go down so she might hide here in this quiet yard forever.

When Jean returned, Karen was trying unsuccessfully to light a cigarette from the pack lying open on the table.

"Here, let me help." Jean struck another match. "Hold the blame thing steady, won't you."

But Karen couldn't keep the cigarette from quivering between her lips. She was watching the smooth brown arm and how white it was on the inside. And she felt still the echoes of Annette's ill humor. Still, she wanted to think about Annette, about anything but herself. Anything.

"Look, if you won't inhale ..." She dropped the burnt match and took the cigarette away. "You'd better give up."

Half laughing, she sat down on the edge of Karen's chair and snapped the cigarette in two. "Hopeless ... hopeless little child." Tearing open the paper, she watched the tobacco sift between her fingers and onto the grass. "Piddling her life away ... hiding ..." She spoke quietly, almost sadly.

"Are you talking about me? Or Annette?"

Jean rested her hand lightly on Karen's leg. "All of us," she said. "Every one of God's chillun."

"You don't seem so hopeless," Karen said, glad to keep the conversation away from herself.

"Ah, but I am."

Karen wanted suddenly to move her leg from under the woman's touch. The skin beneath Jean's palm twinged peculiarly. There was something almost caressing about the way the hand curved. She knew it was all in her own mind, a reaction from the guilt she felt because of the morning's behavior. Yet she did not move, afraid Jean might not understand.

"There is no one in this world who is really hopeless," Karen said, her eyes intently serious.

"But there is. There really is." She leaned back and crossed her legs, leaning one hip against Karen's calf. "It's nothing to be afraid of though. Once you get accustomed to the idea."

"I don't like to hear such things from you."

"Why not?"

Karen took a final sip from her glass and reached out to set it on the umbrellaed table. "Because you're too ... full of life."

"But that's it. That's the hopelessness, you see."

"Oh, Jean, stop playing with me. Please." Her voice sounded strained. Anxious. Too anxious for an afternoon's chat.

Jean nodded obligingly. "All right. What would you rather have me do?"

She felt confused, inane. What indeed did she want Jean to do? Why had she come here? "Oh, I don't know. I don't know. Just talk to me."

Instead of replying immediately, Jean glanced up to follow a sparrow's darting journey from one distant tree to another. "You can stay here as long as you like, you know," she murmured. "Allen has gone off to Daytona Beach. The world is mine. At least for a few weeks."

"I wish I could," Karen sighed. "I really wish I could."

"But you have responsibilities."

Something in Jean's tone put Karen instantly on the defensive. "I have a husband whom I betrayed today," she blurted. She wanted to say more, but the words choked in her throat. She flung herself out of the chair and strode to the opposite end of the garden. A sharp pain jabbed in her chest, as though her lungs were made of jagged bits of metal. She kneeled and bent over one of the heavy-petalled flowers, crumpled now within herself, completely unnerved. The heavy, languid fragrance touched her nostrils and she was glad for it, glad for a spot of beauty in her bleak world. Hot tears rose and spilled over, staining into the curving petals.

Seconds later she sensed Jean's presence, felt the caressing touch again on either arm. The hands steadied her, helped her to her feet.

"I guess you really needed that drink," Jean said.

Karen let herself be taken back into the house. From a cabinet on the screened porch, Jean took out a bottle of Scotch and poured her a double shot.

She drank it straight.

"You can face him," Jean said. "Take it from me. A nice warm bath, a little food in your stomach and this whole mess'll simplify." She held out her hand. "Come on."

Karen had no strength in her to object. She went with Jean into the bathroom, sat docilely while the tub filled, then let Jean undress her. She knew she was being childish. But, at the moment, she wanted to be, wanted to have someone fuss over her and dull the guilt. She sat into the warm water and leaned forward while Jean lathered her back with a fresh cake of pine soap.

"You're really taking this pretty well," Jean said, wringing soapy water from the cloth. "Much better than I did. I made a real scene. Went on a two week binge, with poor Allen looking for me everywhere."

Karen sighed but did not reply.

"I suppose you think it's worse because Steve's flat on his back. Defenseless. There's probably nothing I could say to convince you that you would have done it anyway. Nope, I won't even try. Lean back a little."

Karen leaned back and felt the washcloth slide over her breasts. Jean's words made her uncomfortable, yet she was not at all sure that they weren't true. Nothing made much sense anymore. "I wish I were six years old again," she murmured.

"Who doesn't?" Jean laughed. "Now, stand up and rinse off."

Obediently, Karen stood up while water ran from the spray over her shoulders.

"You'd better put something on those," Jean said clinically and Karen looked to see the blue bruises inside her thighs. "Turn around. Let's see where else you've got 'em."

She felt Jean's fingers running lightly over her flesh.

"Guess that's all," she said. She led Karen onto a white fluffy bathmat and lifted a huge Turkish towel from the rack.

Karen felt her breasts being cupped and lifted. But before she could react, the agile hands had moved downward to her belly, then around to her back, massaging rhythmically, almost hypnotically. All the aching had left her muscles and, for the first time in weeks, she knew she would sleep if she closed her eyes.

"Now get dressed and I'll fix us some supper," Jean said, quietly, not wanting to disturb her mood.

As she dressed, the odor of garlic wafted in from the kitchen and she realized that she was hungry. She had not expected ever to be hungry again. She had thought, somehow, that everything would be changed. Everything.

A fresh salad. Glasses of red wine. Broiled lamb chops on flat white plates. Three bay windows overlooked pine trees and as she sat down, she saw a squirrel's tail whip around a limb.

"It's so lovely here," she breathed. "Seems so far away from … everything."

"Yes," Jean said lightly. "A pleasant delusion. Good for the digestion, at any rate."

It was not till after they had eaten and were busy with the dishes that Jean forced her back to reality. She said, very calmly, "Have you decided what you're going to do?"

Karen held on tightly to the cup in her hand. "No. No. I don't even want to think about it. Tomorrow. I'll think about it tomorrow."

"Karen, listen to me. I don't give a damn if you never think about it again. Believe me." Her green eyes flashed. "But if I'm going to enjoy anything with you, it's got to be with both your eyes wide open."

"I don't see what one thing has to do with another." She let the annoyance show in her voice.

Jean sighed. "You don't see much of anything, my little friend. Do you?"

"Don't trap me, Jean. Please." She picked up a dish from the sinkside. "Do you think I'm enjoying all this? I don't want to run away from Steve. I love him, Jean. I do. I really do."

"Then don't make such a noise about it."

They finished the dishes in silence. It hurt Karen deeply to realize that Jean was not convinced of her devotion to Steve. And for the first time, she felt a niggle of disappointment. Perhaps Jean did not really understand her after all.

Or, perhaps, understood her too well.

"Brooding again?" Jean said when the last dish had been placed on the shelf.

Karen hung up the towel, then turned slowly to face her. "You know, you could be wrong sometimes. I mean ..."

Jean laughed. "Not about you, honey."

"And why not me?"

"Oh," Jean shrugged. "One of those things, I guess."

"You guess nothing. You know. You know what I am and you don't bother giving it fancy names." The lines around her mouth were grim.

"Don't be so hard on yourself," Jean said quietly. "I never called you any names."

"You didn't have to. I know what you think. I'm a thrill kid, that's all. Looking for kicks wherever I can find them." She shook her head dismally. "Somebody else told me that today. And he ought to know."

"Why ought he to know, Karen?"

"Because he's been around a long, long..." Karen stopped abruptly, realizing that she had given away more than she had intended.

Jean examined the few splotches of water on her shorts. "Even the high and mighty can be wrong." She spoke without looking up.

"I appreciate the loyalty, Jean. But it's hopeless. We both know it's true." At the moment, she believed it must be.

"Then you should have no trouble."

Karen raised one dark eyebrow. "What do you mean. I should have no trouble?"

"You can get a divorce with a clear conscience."

Divorce? The word raced through her like a shock. No, she didn't want a divorce. Accident or no accident, she wanted Steve, wanted to be with him, to take care of him. There was something very special in the way she felt about Steve. Something that had nothing to do with sex. Or thrills.

Jean looked at her levelly. "Karen, if you don't want to get a divorce and you're afraid to face him.... Well, just what do you intend to do?"

Karen stared at her dumbly.

"It's all right to be confused. But..." She spread her hands. "Anyhow, let me drive you home. It might help you to be close to the line of attack."

"Oh, no. I couldn't." She felt the fear pulsing into her throat.

"It's got to be, honey."

"Nothing has to be," she said evasively. Yet she knew in her heart that Jean was right. Knew that she must face up to her problem and solve it.

"Come on," Jean prodded. "Play it smart."

And without another word, Karen followed her out to the garage.

CHAPTER FIVE

ALL THE WAY home, Karen worried how she could possibly face the combination of her mother and Steve. Jean's Mercury station wagon sped along the East River Drive, but Jean refused to take her eyes off the road or offer a word of encouragement. Her attitude annoyed Karen, yet she felt she had no right to demand anything more of Jean. She had already done so much to help her.

"Here you go," Jean said, pulling up in front of the apartment house.

There was something in Jean's voice that was out of kilter. Karen sat back and looked at her carefully, trying to find what it was. But before she could pursue it thoroughly, she had an inspiration. She sat up quickly and touched Jean's arm.

"Salvation?" Jean said.

"I think so. Look, will you do me a favor?"

"Hmm?"

"Come along upstairs. They'll both see you and know where I was all day." Jean still wore the polo shirt, but she had fastened a white cotton skirt on over her shorts. She looked well enough dressed.

To Karen's dismay, Jean burst out laughing in a way that seemed to defile her own existence.

"What's so funny about that?" Karen asked with confusion.

"Nothing, honey, nothing," Jean said quickly. And she got out of the car with a sudden nervous movement.

Riding up in the elevator, Karen felt flushes of hot and cold prickle across her skin. Unwittingly, she had put the pieces of her life into Jean's hands. And she was no longer sure they were safe there.

They came into the glimmer of a single light filtering from the living room.

Half hidden in the wing chair, Karen's mother sat erectly behind the rapid clicking of knitting needles. As Karen came in, the woman did not glance up, but seemed to concentrate more intently on her work.

"Hello, Mom," Karen said, kissing her lightly on the forehead. "Has he been much trouble?"

The sentence hung stiffly in the air, waiting to be shattered.

"No trouble 'tall."

The woman's tiny, firm body had always seemed to Karen like a projectile ready to shoot forward and destroy. She reached for Jean's hand, aware of the childish impulse to hide behind her back.

"This is my friend Jean Connors. We spent the day together." She felt as though she were offering Jean, like candy to a guest.

Her mother lay the knitting on her lap and examined Jean closely. "Miss Connors. Or Mrs.?"

"Mrs." The amusement had not yet left Jean's voice. It floated richly, a banner of encouragement in the tense atmosphere.

"In my day, women didn't have time for enjoyin' themselves without their husbands."

Karen's body stiffened with a sense of betrayal. "But you told me to go out," she said defensively. "You've been telling me that for weeks."

"Goin' out is not the same as sprees."

Karen's glance shot guiltily to Jean. She knew better than to retort, for the guilt would sound in her voice, show in her manner.

Jean's smile had begun to subside. "You had neither the time nor the inclination, I imagine." She spoke agreeingly, almost tenderly.

"That's right, young woman." Her gaze seemed to pass through Karen with triumph. Then she folded the piece of work and laid it into a wicker basket. "Steven's asleep but he was grumpy before and I expect he'll be grumpy after, not to say as I blame him. So you'd best watch your toes and fingers." Then she came directly to Jean and shook her hand. "I'll be going. My own supper's still to be cooked."

When Karen had seen her out the door and returned, Jean was standing at the window, her arms folded. She turned as Karen approached and smiled. "Now what was so difficult about that?"

"If she were your mother, you'd know."

"No doubt."

"But I'm grateful just the same. You know that." There was nothing more for Jean to do here. Yet Karen didn't want to let her go. "Jean, I…"

Jean patted Karen lightly on the cheek. "Everything will be just fine, honey. You get some sleep. I'm going home, too."

A lurch of insecurity grabbed at Karen's stomach. She put out a hand to detain Jean, afraid to be left alone just yet with Steve.

"He'll probably sleep through the night," Jean said reassuringly. "And I'll call you first thing in the morning."

Helplessly, Karen sighed.

"You mustn't look so forlorn," Jean grinned. "It's too damn appealing."

And before Karen could say another word, Jean strode across the room and was gone.

She tried to cling to the comfort of Jean's words. Yes, he might sleep through the night. And it was just barely possible that when he did wake up, he would have forgotten.

Possible, not not very probable.

Slumping into the deep cushions of the sofa, she struggled to regain the equilibrium she had felt in Jean's presence. But there was no peace for her, nowhere to turn to escape the guilt. And she listened to the sounds of oncoming darkness, the rumble of trucks heading out to the highway, the faint, high whine of a fire engine. Familiar sounds that she had known when she lay alone and awake in her single bed before Steve. The isolation of those years reached forward to touch her and there was no escaping. She didn't even dare turn on the television set for fear of waking him.

Uncomfortably she began to pace the room. It was hardly eight o'clock. She had a whole night to go.

And then, in the morning, there would be ... Bill. Her heart went cold at the thought.

Regardless of what else happened, Karen knew she had to avoid seeing him again. Not only because of what had already taken place between them. But because she knew she might not be able to resist him. Still, how could she manage not to see him? He had to examine Steve. She didn't dare switch doctors in the middle of everything. There were too many shrewd people in her life. Or suspicious ones.

Hardly realizing her action, Karen went to the liquor cabinet. She poured half a glass of bourbon and raised it to her lips, eyes shut tight. Even in her imagination, she didn't want to see Bill. She could never love him as she loved Steve. Never. And without the love, the union of their bodies seemed cheap and shabby. She drank deeply, on a single breath, immersing herself in the burning sensation, desirous of any feeling, any thought that could drive a wedge between her body and Bill's.

As she gulped and coughed on the whisky, the tinkling of Steve's bell came to her. Alerted, she set down the glass and listened. It rang again, louder this time, more persistent.

Karen's hand went to her hair. She pushed back the careless straggles from her temples and cleared her throat. But the taste and the odor did not go away. Facing Steve in this condition meant certain accusation. She flinched from the insistent tinkle. Yet she had to go to him.

"Put on the light," he said as she tried to tiptoe in.

"Won't it be too hard on your eyes, dear?"

"Since when do you give a damn about my eyes?"

She flicked the switch and stood holding onto the door jamb uncertainly. "What can I get for you?" Her voice came out high and tight, hardly her own.

"A couple of aspirins. My head aches, thinkin' about you all day." He squinted at her, shading his eyes with the drooping pajama sleeve. "I didn't think you'd have the guts to get that old witch to come stay with me. You must've been pretty anxious to get away from here."

His tone was cruel and cutting. Yet Karen recognized something different about him now, a hopelessness that seemed to echo her own feelings. She stepped to the bureau for the bottle of pills and unscrewed the cap. Her hands moved a little more steadily.

"I needed a breath of fresh air, that's all." She stood half turned away from him, still afraid to face him squarely.

"I guess anybody would after all this time." He touched the edge of his hair with his palm. "If I could get out a little, even onto a porch..." He shrugged resignedly.

She brought him the pills and a glass of water. "I know, darling." She spoke gently, yet her mind raced with confusion. This sudden return of his good nature was something she couldn't fight, couldn't maneuver.

"Sit down with me for a minute. I want to talk to you."

As he touched her wrist, Karen felt a cold, miserable perspiration break out like hives on her back. She had imagined how terrible it would be to face his nasty accusations. But this? What was she supposed to do against this all-too-human need for commiseration? She couldn't even run from it.

She sat down cautiously on the chair beside the bed and waited.

He swallowed the pills and the water. "I guess I owe you an apology."

She saw him hanging onto the glass as she had been hanging onto the bottle of bourbon only a few moments before. Her whole being ached for him, yet she could not tell him so. "Steve, don't," she murmured, wanting to tell him to shout at her, to call her the names she deserved. To ease the guilt a little by hating her.

"I meant it," he said sincerely. "There was no excuse. I love you. I know you love me. And what the hell I was trying to prove, I'll never know."

"You mustn't," her voice choked on the words.

"But I want to. All afternoon I was lying here, thinking how much I must've hurt you to drive you out of the house like that. You know, I wanted to cry because I couldn't run after you and bring you back. I wanted you to know I'm sorry." He put out his palm for her hand. "Sit closer."

She pulled the chair in toward the bed and felt his warm fingers circle her chill ones.

"It's going to be all right," he continued. "I don't know why I thought Bill might be kidding me along. No self-confidence, I guess. You know how it is when you've been flat on your back? It's like death warmed over. You get all kinds of crazy ideas." He frowned thoughtfully for a moment. Then he looked full at her and smiled with more energy than she'd seen from him since before the accident. "Come sit on the bed here."

She couldn't bring herself to move. Yet she knew she must. She had to keep him from the least suspicion. Especially now. "Let me put out the light first," she whispered so he could not tell the quiver in her voice. "It's so much nicer together in the dark."

She got the light off and returned to poise gingerly on the edge of the mattress. She held herself tightly together, barely within his reach.

"Hey," he said teasingly, "you playing hard to get?"

She laughed and tried to make it sound casual. Then she leaned toward him as his arm went around her waist, pulling her closer, directing her to lie down beside him.

What was he trying to do? She sensed something urgent about his movements, something demanding. Yet they both knew that he couldn't ...

She closed her eyes and lay still, letting his hand move over her body as he wished. Anything, anything to placate him.

"It's gonna be just like old times again," he said hoarsely.

As he spoke, his hand wandered warmly down the length of her thigh. He began to stroke her leg as she had known him to do preliminary to their love making. Horrified, she tried to remain perfectly still. Yet she felt the craving start deep inside her as it always did when Steve touched her like this. Her skin tingled beneath his fingers and she knew he must sense it, too.

"Poor kid," he muttered. "All wound up. There's no reason why we can't take care of it for you. Where there's love ... what difference does it make how?"

He spoke with his lips against the side of her throat. She felt the vapor of his breath move inside the V-neck of her dress. His fingers had begun to tug up the hem of her skirt.

"Darling," she stroked his forehead. "You mustn't exert yourself." Her hand moved to stop the exploring fingers. "We can wait."

Ignoring her attempt to ward him off, his hand had crept beneath her dress and moved up along the inside of her thigh. Searching, probing the part of her he knew so well. "Why should you wait? When it's so easy ... so easy to ... take the edge off?"

"Not that way." With all the strength she could muster, Karen pulled away from him and pushed the skirt between her knees protectively. "I don't want it that way, darling. Either it's both of us ... or nobody."

She heard a deep breath release from him.

"You mean that?" he said.

"Of course I do."

He lay back against the pillow and folded his hands on his chest. "Thank God for that. I was beginning to think it was getting out of control."

She couldn't say anything but sat there, stroking his forehead and feeling hot barbs of agony sear through her insides. All of her had been aroused in the few moments of their intimacy, all of her yearned toward fulfillment. Yet she sensed somehow that Steve did not really understand, that he resented her need. And she was glad now that she had not let him make love to her.

When he touched her again, cupping his hand behind her head, smoothing her hair, there was no leap of response, but a vast expanse of frustration and hurt.

"Hey, what's with you, anyhow?" His voice was quiet, almost sad. "You said it's okay."

She sat up away from him and held his hand in her lap. "I was just…" She tilted her head to smile at him. What, after all, could she say? What could she possibly achieve by telling him the truth?

She brought his fingers to her lips and kissed them gently. "I was remembering how very much I love you. And feeling a little guilty that you'd been worrying about me. Heaven knows, you've had enough to contend with, without my adding to it."

Steve shifted a little against the pillows and she leaned forward to make the backrest more comfortable.

"I'm not blaming you for anything," he said. "I know it's my own filthy mind."

Suddenly she wanted to laugh and cry, all at the same time. His filthy mind? God help them both. The memory of the morning's episode with Bill rushed in on her with stark, hideous clarity. The way he had grabbed her… And she had responded with the furious, panting need of a bitch in heat. Her cheeks burned now with the memory of it. The nerve began to pulse in her right temple.

She knew Steve was waiting, wanting her to say something, anything to justify his confidence in her. Needing her to have faith in him, now that he had none in himself. Yet she could not bring herself to meet his eyes, afraid that he might see in hers the guilty secret he must never know.

"I really didn't do much of anything," she said, sitting beside him on the bed, speaking casually, but to a spot somewhere above his head. "I went to Bill's office for some sleeping pills, then roamed through the zoo for a while. Then," she raised one shoulder easily, "I went up to the Bronx to visit Jean." She listened to herself drone on, describing the home Steve had never seen, mentioning Annette. Being chatty, friendly, as she had always been with him before the accident.

Obviously he believed her, for she sensed him relaxing, settling down more comfortably under the sheet. He didn't interrupt and when she glanced at him, she saw the hint of a smile tugging at one corner of his mouth.

"You're smiling," she said.

"Hm hmm. At me. I'm a first class jerk sometimes. I should've known it was something like that." His head nodded sleepily.

Without answering, Karen stood up and pulled the sheet up snugly around him. "You get some sleep," she said. "Bill will be here early tomorrow." She kissed him lightly on the forehead and began to back away toward the door.

"Don't go," he mumbled.

She wanted to go off somewhere and hide. Yet she had come this far safely and she knew that she dare not make a mistake now.

She sat on the chair by his bed and rested her hand on his arm. "I'm here," she whispered.

She stayed stiffly in the darkness beside him until he was sleeping soundly. Then she tiptoed out and down the hall.

In the living room she poured herself another drink. A long one. She lay down on the sofa without bothering to undress and closed her eyes. Every nerve in her body screamed with pain. The elevator door clanged shut out in the hail. Spike heels clicked across the floor in the apartment next door. The air was heavy with the sound of his sleeping.

She fell finally into a fitful doze.

The doorbell had been ringing sharply for several moments before she reached the foyer. She opened the door an inch and peered out, then flung it wide. Bill stood there, staring at her, pleading with her, his eyes dull with desire. He didn't say a word. He didn't have to.

She led him inside to the couch. His lips found hers hungrily, his hands caressed her breasts, gently, then more roughly. He forced her down to the couch and her legs spread wide to welcome him. She reached out to touch him and led him to her.

And it happened, the way she wanted it. Hard and good. She felt herself floating, floating...

She sat up shaking, drenched with perspiration. She felt depleted, her limbs heavy with sleep...and something else. A dream. Yet not a dream, for she recognized the ragged incompleteness she sensed for what it was.

I must be sick, she thought wildly. *I can't even trust myself with myself any more.*

She got off the couch and began to pace the length of the room. And back again. Slowly, slowly, trying to get a grip on herself. Afraid to take another drink. Afraid to sleep. Caught up in a misery that knew no comfort, that could find no relief.

For she knew that she loved Steve and wanted him and that, because she did, she must wait. He could not stand the shame of having forced her to seek another man, and therefore he had blinded himself to the true strength of her need. She must not be unfaithful to him again or she could not live with him nor with herself.

Yet.... How long could she wait, how long deny the aching need within her?

Karen stood by the window, gloomily watching another dawn spread over the city.

CHAPTER SIX

WHEN THE PHONE rang at eight-thirty, Karen was still standing by the window, engrossed with the riddle of her future. She had concentrated on her problem for hours, examining the situation from every possible aspect. She knew that she would never again be unfaithful to Steve. That she would face Bill calmly this morning and, if need be, reject him. Yet her nerves told her that she must seek another outlet for the energies consuming her.

The insistent buzz of the phone caught her attention finally and she moved swiftly toward it. Her head throbbed with each step. Her eyes grated in their sockets. Almost angrily, she scooped up the phone and pressed it to her ear.

Jean's voice at the other end sounded sleepy and intimate, yet full of the usual good-natured banter. As she listened, Karen let herself relax against the wall by the telephone table. Her long fingers worked futilely to smooth the wrinkles out of her skirt.

"Of course I'm all right," she said to Jean's question. She kept her voice low so that Steve might not hear. "But, believe me, I've learned my lesson. From now on, I stay right here where I belong. No more ..."

Jean's throaty laugh cut her off short. Something about it blatantly accused her of being absurd. Or childish.

"What's so funny this time?" she said irritably. "I begin to feel like all you do is laugh at me."

"Hardly," Jean answered easily. "It's simply that I find you delightful."

"But ..." Karen protested.

Jean cut her off again. "Forget it," she said. "But remember this: I'm home most of the time. So, when you need a place to run to..."

After she'd hung up, Karen stood for a long time staring at the phone, trying to make some kind of sense out of her friend's behavior. It was like Jean to laugh. At everything. Yet Jean had been more than willing to do all she could to help last evening. Didn't she understand that the help Karen really needed now was a little moral support?

Finally Karen shrugged impatiently and went off to the bathroom to make herself presentable. Steve would be awake at any moment, if he wasn't already. She had a lot to make up to him for. Not only for Bill. But for herself, her thoughts, her lack of trust. He didn't deserve that from her.

And he certainly didn't deserve the ghastly appearance peering back at her from the mirror. Her face was pale and drawn, almost haggard, the skin under her eyes puffy and charcoal gray. She opened the medicine cabinet and lined an array of make-up across the back of the sink. With a white pencil, she went to work on the pouches under her eyes.

As she applied her mask, her thoughts drifted again to Steve. Steve, who depended on her. Who loved and trusted her. And whom she had betrayed. It did not help Karen at all to realize that she had managed to get away with her deception. Indeed, it made matters worse. For she would have to live with the guilt, clutching it to her, letting it gnaw at her in the quiet hours. Already the ravages of it showed on her face. Surely he would see. And know.

There was no way out for her. No way to stifle the craving of her flesh, no way to hide the guilt. And, though she loved him, she began to feel that he might be better off without her. For her very being must scream at him his failure, his inadequancy as a man. She knew he had not yet allowed himself to see her as she had become since the accident. That he had not dared. But he could not blind himself forever.

She pulled the comb quickly through her hair. She hadn't bothered to set it and it hung limply in loose strands. She pulled it in tightly at the nape of her neck and caught it with a silver clasp.

All in all, she looked a little like a zombie in a crumpled shroud, she decided. She felt even worse. But she forced herself to stand up straight and set a stiff little smile across her lips. Then she strode quickly to the bedroom, to see if he were ready for breakfast.

"Well, hi," he said warmly.

He held out his arms and she went into them gladly, hiding her face against his neck. He brushed her cheek with his chin and the bristles were rough and sweet against her skin. He held her so tightly, so surely that for a moment she almost forgot the truth, the ugly truth of what their marriage had become.

His palm circled on her breast, bringing the nipple instantly to a hard, pulsating point of life. His mouth caressed the hollow of her throat.

Caught completely off guard, Karen surrendered herself willingly to the pleasurable sensations shivering through her. Without thinking, without caring, she let him explore intimately. His hand moved beneath her dress, tugged clumsily at her panties. Her body trembled against his.

She raised her hips to make it easier for him. He didn't need any help. He pulled her on top of him, his hand already moving beneath her clothing.

As he touched her, Karen sucked in her breath sharply. His mouth met hers hard, his tongue darted between her teeth. His hand moved slowly, slowly. She jerked convulsively and he stepped up the pace.

She felt the familiar, crazy aching sensation in the pit of her stomach, the muscles tightening along the insides of her thighs. And just when she thought she could bear it no longer, her knees tightened around him like a vise, then released as she climbed toward fulfillment.

Then she lay quiet on top of him, feeling neither peace nor satisfaction, but a nagging sense of incompleteness. No matter what anybody said, it just wasn't the same thing. It was almost like when she sometimes tried satisfying herself. It felt good, but only aggravated the need.

Yet she couldn't let Steve know this. Ever. It might be all he could do for her, at least for a long time to come. It would be enough. It had to be.

She kissed him gently on the mouth and rolled away from him. He had a triumphant smirk in his eyes that she couldn't bear to look at. She got off the bed slowly, deliberately using her body as though it throbbed with pleasure instead of pain. As he watched her, she stepped out of the wrinkled dress and took a fresh one from the closet.

She felt him watching her closely, waiting for her, and she was afraid suddenly to turn and face him. What was she supposed to say, now that it was over? Now that her failure was complete?

Her slip caught in the zipper. "Damn," she exploded. Couldn't anything go right this morning?

"Let me do it," he said.

She sat beside him on the bed so he could reach the zipper. "I should have taken a shower, I suppose," she said. "But Bill will be here any minute and…"

"Yeah, I know," he mumbled. "I should've waited." He grinned at her lecherously. "But that's how it is sometimes." He gave a tug at the zipper and it slid up easily. "There."

She touched the top of his crew cut with her palm. "You don't hear any complaints, do you?"

"Seriously," he said and his eyes were deeply serious. "I heard you get up in the middle of the night."

"I'm sorry," she said quickly.

"No. I was awake myself. Thinking about us." He sighed tiredly. "Even though everything seemed to be all right, I … Well, I knew it couldn't be right for you. I mean, you're only human.

And God knows it's not your fault that I'm ..." he gestured at his sheet covered body, "... out of commission."

She smiled and put two fingers under his chin and tilted his lips to hers. "I love you," she murmured against his mouth. "More than you'll ever know."

"I do know. That's why ..."

"Oh, darling. I meant it when I said we could wait. If you hadn't caught me off guard this morning, why, I would hardly have given it a thought," she lied glibly.

He tilted an eyebrow questioningly.

"Not that I'm not happy you did," she added hastily.

She saw the suspicion and the distrust creeping back into his eyes and she knew instantly that she had already said too much. Yet somehow she couldn't shut herself off and she heard her voice, too high and too nervous, babbling on about nothing and everything. She had to let him believe that she found him adequate, that she always would. Yet she felt no conviction in what she was saying and the words echoed hollowly in her ears.

Please, God, help me, she prayed silently. *Don't let me hurt him any more than I already have.*

Steve made no comment on her monologue, but she sensed him stiffen and draw away from her. She pretended not to notice. But her hands, clasped tightly in her lap, were trembling and felt slimy with perspiration.

She had never been so thankful for anything as she was for the sound of the doorbell when it finally came. After this episode, nothing could ever perturb her again. Not even Bill.

She got up quickly and smoothed out her skirt. "That must be the doctor," she said lightly. And she was out of the room before he could say a word.

When she opened the door to Bill, it didn't happen at all the way it had been in her dream. He simply took off his hat and stood smiling at her until she moved aside to let him enter. He turned in the center of the living room and waited for her to join him.

"How's the patient?" he asked.

"Oh, he's fine," Karen said. "He hasn't had breakfast yet, but he seems pretty chipper." She forced herself to meet Bill's gaze steadily, almost defiantly. "He's waiting for you."

Bill shook his head slowly. "I wasn't referring to Steve," he said quietly. "I know all about his condition." He put his hands on her shoulders and held her at arms' length. "I meant you, my dear. You obviously haven't slept. I daresay you haven't filled the prescription I gave you."

His expression showed sincere concern and she swallowed the nasty words that had leaped onto her tongue. After all, she couldn't really blame Bill. She had gone to him for help. His treatment may have been somewhat unprofessional, but it had been effective nevertheless.

No, she had nothing to blame but her own wantonness. She glanced away from him, her cheeks hot with shame.

"None of that," he said softly. He moved close to her, his arms going around her. He held her gently, like a big brother. "What's done is just that and nothing more."

"I'm so ashamed," she whispered. "I can't help that."

"I hope you won't hate me."

"I don't hate you, Bill. It's myself I can't stand." She sighed. "It's not pleasant to see yourself for what you really are."

"It never is," he said. He stepped away from her and bent to retrieve the little black bag. "I'd like to talk with you when I've finished examining Steve."

She looked at him questioningly.

"It's important, Karen."

She nodded. "I'll put up some coffee."

In the kitchen she ran water into a tea kettle and set it up to boil. She spooned coffee into the top of the pot and got down cups, saucers and napkins. She handled the things clumsily, making unnecessary noise that jarred her already shattered nerves.

What could Bill possibly want to speak with her about? Surely he must understand there could be no repetition of yesterday's episode. Even if he did not approve of her remorse, as a friend he must know that she was suffering and respect that fact.

Or maybe he had news about Steve's condition. Maybe there had been some new discovery, some development that could help Steve. Surgeons were doing such remarkable things these days. Maybe... An injured spinal nerve. It sounded so nothing, yet meant so much. And in her heart Karen knew there would be no miracle cure for Steve. Just rest and patience. And hope.

And for herself? What cure could anyone offer her?

The kettle began its tremulous whistle. She lifted it quickly off the stove and poured the boiling water into the top of the coffee pot.

Remembering Steve, his changing moods, the way he had made love to her, Karen realized that she would be better off with nothing than with the half satisfaction she had experienced. She was not quite sure what had made Steve change his attitude during the night. But she sensed that it had very little to do with love. More likely, it had been Steve's way of asserting himself with her, of making sure she still belonged to him and always would.

Her thoughts reeled crazily across her brain till she pressed her hands to her temples to quiet them. If only she could get away for a little while, really get away, where she could sit down and think this thing through clearly.

But even that was impossible. She could hardly walk out and leave Steve alone.

"Coffee ready?"

Karen started violently and spun to face him. "Bill, you frightened me," she said, half-apologetically for she knew he must think her a fool. "I'll bring it into the living room in just a moment."

"Let's have it here." He sat down into one of the chairs by the kitchen table.

She knew he had chosen to remain in the kitchen to be sure that Steve could not hear them. But she made no objection. She brought two steaming cups to the table and sat down across from him.

"How is he?"

"Fine. Just as I said earlier." He took a sip of the hot coffee. Then he set the cup down and folded his hands on the table in front of him. "Now that that's settled, let's get down to cases, shall we?"

Her eyes widened. "What cases?"

"I'll put it bluntly," he said. "I think this job is getting to be a little more than you're able to handle alone. I've arranged for a sleep-in nurse. She'll be here sometime late this afternoon."

Karen felt as though she had just been slapped in the face. She set the cup she was holding very carefully into its saucer. "Go on."

He shrugged. "There isn't much else to say, really. Her name is Lila Proctor and I've known her for years. She's quite competent. And she's had a great deal of experience with cases similar to Steve's."

His words made no sense to her. None at all. "But why, Bill? Why? I thought we agreed from the first that I would be the best nurse for Steve. He's told you himself that he doesn't want anyone else."

"True," he admitted. "But, as I explained to Steve, we'll be starting therapy in a week or two. He'll need a trained person around to help him. Of course it could be done at a clinic. But he's not ready for all that travelling just yet. Besides," he spread his hands on the table top and lowered his glance from hers, "I think you could use a little time off. Steve agrees with me."

"You told Steve that?"

"Yes, I did."

"I suppose you also told him what you think I should do with my free time," her voice rose angrily. "Did he agree with that, too, Bill?"

He leaned across the table and covered her trembling hands with his own steady ones. "What you do with your time is entirely up to you, Karen. You might even try catching up on your sleep," he added gently.

"Oh, Bill, I'm sorry." She felt her lips quivering with incipient tears. "I'm so sorry. I don't know what's come over me lately."

The tears welled up and spilled over. She put her face between her hands and sobbed now freely.

Almost instantly he was beside her. He gripped her by the arms and pulled her up against him. Tenderly he stroke her hair, soothingly. She let herself relax in his arms, needing the comfort and the warmth. He gave her a handkerchief and she dabbed at her eyes.

"Better?"

"A little," she sniffed. "I'm ashamed to act like this in front of you, Bill."

"Why?"

"Oh ..." She started to say because he was an outsider. But he wasn't really. He had known her even longer than Steve had, knew her probably as well as anyone could.

He didn't wait for her to finish. His arms went about her tightly, lifting her off the floor. His lips pressed bruisingly down on hers. His hands cupped under her buttocks and he ground himself insistently, demandingly into her.

For a full minute she was caught up in the hot fever of her desire. Then, as his fingers fumbled at the neck of her dress, she remembered yesterday. And Steve, waiting down the hall in the bedroom for his loving wife.

She put both her hands on his chest and thrust herself away from him.

He stood looking down at her wordlessly and, she thought, contemptuously.

"Don't you ever try that again." She spat the words at him furiously. "And don't think I'll come running to you just because you've arranged it so I'll have free time."

Bill raised his shoulders then and nonchalantly spread his hands. "Why not?" he said. "If it's not me, it will be someone else. Where will you go, Karen? Into the streets, the bars?"

"To my husband," she said triumphantly.

He started to smile.

"Laugh, if you will," she said. "He has already proved himself quite capable." She smiled. "You wouldn't understand about that, Bill. But when two people love each other, there are always ways…"

And now he laughed aloud, his head thrown back, his amusement obviously sincere.

"Damn you," she breathed. She could have slain him on the spot. Instead, she turned away from him and went to the sink and stood there, clinging to the metal edging.

He came up behind her, but did not try to touch her. "I'm sorry for that," he said. "But I know you too well, my girl. You can't be satisfied with children's games. You need the real thing."

His words seared into her brain, condemning her with their blunt, pitiful truth. Her shoulders slumped dismally as the last ounce of fight went out of her.

He pecked her lightly on the back of the neck. "I'll be expecting you," he said. "Any time."

When she turned around, he was gone.

CHAPTER SEVEN

AS SHE SET out his breakfast things on the tray, Karen realized that she did not enjoy the prospect of facing Steve after what she had just been through. It was bad enough that she had made a fool of herself in front of Bill. Even worse, she had to admit he had been right. If she could not maintain the pose of the satisfied wife with an outsider, how could she hope to convince Steve?

She put two slices of buttered toast on a plate and covered it to keep it warm. It had been a point of pride with her that his meals were always tasty and attractively served. Yet this morning she realized that the care she took with the tray was a matter of habit more than concern. The awareness startled her with its frank appraisal of her selfishness. She had let herself become immersed in her own suffering, forgetting that Steve was surely worse off than she.

She felt hot points of shame blossom on her skin and quickly she lifted the tray and started toward the bedroom. As she walked, she forced herself to relax and the smile she had ready for him was almost sincere.

Steve sat propped against the pillows, his head turned toward the window. He did not bother to look around as she entered the room.

"Breakfast is served," she said lightly. She could not see the expression on his face. But his shoulders slumped dismally. "Nice fresh shad roe. Eggs. Coffee ..."

"Leave it," he said. "I'm not hungry right now."

"But it's already two hours past breakfast time."

"I said, leave it." He looked straight at her now, his eyes bleak, his complexion more sallow than ever.

"All right," she said quietly. She set the tray carefully on the table beside his bed. "If that's the way you want it, I'll leave it."

He held out a hand toward her. "Look, I didn't mean to yell at you. It's just … Well, I've got a lot of thinking to do, that's all."

Karen knew without his explaining that he was thinking about Bill, about the nurse who was coming, about herself. And she knew, too, that he would have plenty to yell about later, when he had finished with the thinking. Yet she felt trapped, for there was nothing she could do, nothing she could say to reassure him. A man who was no longer a man must of necessity be suspicious and afraid.

She sighed and bent to plant a kiss firmly on top of his bristly soft head. "All right," she said. "I'll leave you alone. If you need anything …"

"I don't need anything," he said bitterly. He turned slowly to face the window again. "I've got everything a man could possibly want."

She knew the situation with him was hopeless. She had no choice but to let him alone, to worry, to warp, to distort the situation to fill whatever need for self-punishment he suffered. Gently, she tucked the sheet in around his shoulders. Then she left him without another word.

When she reached the living room, Karen paused and looked around her, wondering what she could possibly find to do that might distract her from her own worries. She didn't want to think about herself anymore. Nor about Steve. She didn't want to think about anything. Not now.

Yet what was she supposed to do in this house she no longer thought of as a home? She had cleaned till the place was spotless. The laundry had already been sent out for the week. There was a frying pan dirty in the sink, but it hardly seemed worth the effort. She felt useless here. Useless and not really even wanted.

Abruptly she cut off the flow of negative thoughts trying to flood into her consciousness. In her desire to pamper herself, to feel sorry for herself, she had completely forgotten about the nurse Bill was sending to move in with them. Welcome or not, the woman had to be made comfortable.

Karen stopped at the linen closet long enough to pick up sheets and towels, then hurried down the hall to Steve's den. A small but cozy room, it was the one spot in the apartment Karen avoided as much as she could. For in this room were displayed the trophies, the ribbons, the photographs Steve had accumulated during his racing days. And she could not bear to see them and be reminded of the past.

Carefully avoiding the mantel and its proud display of silver cups, Karen made up a bed for Miss Lila Proctor on the wide, foam rubber couch. It was a man's room, with its wood panelled walls and deep leather chairs. Yet the couch seemed comfortable enough. She would stand a large bouquet on the table between the windows. That might help a little to add the touch of softness every woman craved.

After she had brought in the flowers from the living room, Karen stepped back and surveyed the finished project critically, deciding that she certainly could be comfortable here. Miss Proctor, as a live-in nurse, had probably made herself comfortable in places not nearly so pleasant as this.

As she turned to leave the room, her glance touched a leather framed photograph on Steve's desk. And she smiled, remembering the circumstances under which it had been taken. Two weeks before the accident, when Steve had set a new speed record and she had been waiting for him in the pit. He had grabbed her and kissed her as though they were alone, instead of surrounded by admiring fans, and one of Steve's buddies had snapped a picture of their embrace.

Her eyes clouded with tears as she picked up the photograph. That had been just six weeks ago. Six weeks. Yet it seemed to her that it must have been in another lifetime. They had been so happy together then, so completely absorbed in each other. And now, there was nothing left between them but bitterness and regret. Why had they failed each other now, when they needed each other most?

The more she stared at the picture, the more convinced Karen became that the fault was entirely her own. After all, she had been behaving like a juvenile, as though the whole world would come to an end if she didn't have everything just the way she wanted it. She had closed her heart to hope, to love, to understanding. To everything positive.

And here she stood now, like a fool, with tears in her eyes for the past and not one good thought for the future. How stupid!

She pulled open the center drawer of the desk and lay the photograph face down on the bottom. Then she wiped away the tears from her cheek with the back of her hand. Holding herself very straight, she hurried out to the kitchen and ran hot water into the sink.

As long as she could manage to keep herself busy, Karen knew she could manage to stave off the creeping paralysis of fear. And if she herself could be genuinely cheerful and creative in her approach to life, then surely some of it would communicate to Steve. No wonder he had been afraid of losing her. She had been acting as though he already had. But there would be no more time for that. Now that he was about to begin therapy, there would be plenty for them both to do. Soon he would be out of bed. Maybe for a while on crutches. But he would be able to go outdoors soon. They would go for walks together. Like before ...

And maybe, in time, there would even be ...

But she had promised herself not to think about that and she cut the thought off quickly.

By three o'clock she had washed the few dishes, watered the plants, run the sweeper over the immaculate carpet and scrubbed the bathroom for the fourth time in a week. She made a fresh pot of coffee and sat down in the kitchen with a steaming cupful before her. She felt pleasantly tired, which she recognized as an unusual sensation, for she had been suffering only nervous exhaustion and tension for weeks. And the sensation satisfied her, for it seemed to her a sign of progress.

She sipped at the hot coffee and felt the warmth of it spread through her languidly, easing her tired limbs, soothing her. All of her felt good, confident, fulfilled. And when at three-thirty Steve's bell finally summoned her, she fairly ran down the hall to his room.

"When's that damned nurse supposed to get here?" he threw at her as she entered.

The tone of his voice drew her up short and she approached the bed almost cautiously. "I don't really know," she answered. "Bill said late this afternoon. Why?"

He shrugged. "Well, I'm thirsty. And now that you've resigned from the job..."

Karen gripped the edge of the night table and clung to it as though for her very life. So that's how it was going to be. She might have expected something like this. She had been so carried away by her own high spirits that she had forgotten he had been lying here brooding all afternoon.

But this time she was determined that she was not going to be overwhelmed by his mood. A whole future depended on her behavior now. Their future.

She managed to keep her voice pleasant. "Oh, I think I might be able to manage it," she said easily. "At least until she gets here."

She felt him watching her as she poured the water.

When she brought the glass toward his lips, Steve grabbed her wrist and held it. "You think it's funny?" he said hoarsely. "How the hell would you like it, lyin' here thinkin' I'd run out on you?"

"If I were lying there," she said quietly, "I wouldn't think any such thing. I'd know better."

He swallowed a few gulps of the water and pushed away the glass. "It's easy for you to say that. You never ..." He made a gesture of disgust with his hand.

"That's true," she admitted. Very carefully she set the glass down beside the vacuum pitcher and wiped away a drop of water with the tip of one finger. It was difficult to find the right words to say to him. Especially now, when he was feeling so defensive. No matter what she said, he would twist it to fit his own conclusions. Still, she couldn't very well just leave it like this.

She balanced herself on the edge of the mattress, not really putting all her weight on it, yet needing the security of a firm surface beneath her. "I have a pretty good idea of what's going through your mind," she said slowly. "But ... Well, please try to remember that the nurse was Bill's idea, not mine. I was every bit as surprised as you were."

He made a nasty sound in his throat. "Yeah, I'll bet."

"No, really," she insisted.

"Look, what kind of fool do you think I am? He wouldn't of come up with this if you hadn't been griping."

She knew he would make it unpleasant for both of them. She could hear the hurt, the anger and the resentment in his voice. Yet she did not try to stop or contradict him.

"Not that I blame you," he went on. "I'm bored out of my damned skull and I guess you must be, too. But I didn't think you'd have the gall to do this."

"To do what?" she said as calmly as she could.

"To get me a keeper so you can go out whorin' around," he said nastily.

"Oh, Steve."

"Don't 'Oh Steve' me. I fell for your line once, kid. But no more. Do ya think I don't know what you were doin' yesterday?"

"You should. I told you myself."

"Bull," he muttered. "You were out gettin' laid, that's what. No wonder you were so damned pious. 'We can wait,'" he mimicked. "Sure you could wait. The hell with what I wanted. You already had yours."

Karen felt waves of heat rush through her. She felt as though she might faint. But it was not shame and guilt she felt now. It was rage. For she realized that Steve did not really care what she had done. He wanted only to justify himself, to blame her for everything, as he had tried to do before. And for this she almost hated him. As long as he refused to take responsibility for his part of their relationship, there could be no hope for their future together.

Still, only this afternoon had she begun to accept her own share of the responsibility. She must give him time.

"I'm sorry if you believe that," she said gently. "I thought it would be better for you if we did wait. That's all."

"What the hell do you think I am, a vegetable? I'm still a man, Karen, and don't you ever forget it."

"I haven't," she said. She touched his hand lightly. "You proved that this morning." She kept her voice low, throaty.

He looked as though she'd thrown a bucket of ice water into his face. And like he wanted to strangle her for doing it. She got up off the bed and strode to the window. She stood with her back toward him, her hands clenched into tight fists on the sill.

"I'll tell you a secret," she said to the window, but loudly enough for him to hear. "I *will* be glad to get out of this house now and then. Before I go insane." She spun now to face him. "Don't you see what you're doing, Steve. Don't you?"

He was looking at her, but she couldn't be sure he was even listening. His face had gone white and the skin around his eyes looked puffy and old.

"Every half hour you're in a different mood. And most of them are unbearable." She watched his eyes and knew she should stop before she carried this thing too far. Yet she caught a quick breath and plunged on. "I'm beginning to believe that you hate me. I can't get close to you at all anymore. Not at all. I need to know that I'm wanted, Steve. Every woman needs that."

"Look, goddammit, you know I can't..."

"I didn't mean that," she interrupted quickly. "I mean, wanted as a person. As me."

"You know I love you."

She paused thoughtfully. "No," she said finally. "I'm not even sure of that anymore. I thought so a little while ago, but..." She bit her lip and glanced away from him. "When...when you made love to me this morning, it wasn't because you wanted me, Steve. It was because you had to prove to yourself that you are still a man."

He said nothing, but she sensed something ugly in the way he looked at her now. She had always been afraid of his anger before. Yet now she felt the stir of an emotion she had never expected to have toward him, something very like contempt. And she knew that as long as Steve could not respect himself, she would find it almost impossible to do so either.

Still, she loved him. She truly did. And she felt ashamed and sorry for what had been happening between them. It was too late now to go back and try to start over. But she had to make one final attempt.

"Please listen to me, Steve. You must understand. I love you enough to wait forever, if we have to." She raised her chin defiantly, at the moment believing sincerely that she meant every word of what she was saying. "But I just can't go on like this. It's making a nervous wreck out of me. Out of both of us."

When he spoke, his voice was cold, tautly controlled. "When did you make up this pretty little speech, Karen?"

She went suddenly chill all over, hearing the contempt she had felt for him being directed now at herself.

"You don't love me," he said positively. "You got over that the day I cracked up. All you ever wanted from me was a little excitement, a few thrills. Don't think I don't know your story. You want to be wanted, you say? What a laugh!"

"What do you mean?"

"I mean you're a cheap, lyin' bitch, that's what I mean. I've wanted you like nobody else ever could, Karen. I wanted you this morning that way. Because I love you."

She heard the strange, almost whining tone in his voice. Heard it and knew he had not really understood a word she had said to him. She had not realized the extent to which he had been able to delude himself to shift the blame unto her for all their troubles. Yet she knew it now. And she had to face it now. Face it and accept her own defeat.

"I can't fight you anymore," she said calmly. "What would you like me to do?"

He snorted disgustedly. "What the hell difference does it make what I want? All I ever wanted from you was a little love and understanding. But you can't give me that. You can't give me anything."

She stood away from the windowsill and held herself rigidly erect, her head high. "Would you like me to leave?" she asked quietly.

"Oh, sure. You'd like that now, wouldn't you? Then you could do anything you please and not have to feel guilty." He propped himself up high on the pillows. He looked at her now with hatred in his eyes. "You're not goin' anywhere or I'll break your damned neck. You're still my wife."

She held herself tightly together, trying to choke back the sob rising to her throat. "I thought perhaps you had forgotten that," she said. "You've been treating me more like the local prostitute."

She saw him flush angrily, the color creeping into his cheeks, his neck bulging with fury. For a long moment he simply glared at her. Then he looked away.

She knew she had lost him.

"Get the hell out of here" his voice came low and full of hatred. "And stay out."

She started to protest. "But you just said ..."

His head whirled toward her. "I don't care what I just said. You're not worth it."

She took a step toward him, her hand extended. "Steve, you don't mean that."

"Keep away from me," he warned.

"I just wanted to..." She thought quickly. "...to fix the blanket."

"Leave it."

Suddenly she could not bear the tension for another moment. Tears rose to her eyes and spilled onto her cheeks. She flung herself toward him, needing for him to hold her, to tell her that he wanted and needed her.

He caught her by the shoulders and flung her cruelly away from him.

Her hip grazed the edge of the night table. Too shocked to speak she stood rubbing the bruised hip, watching him and waiting.

He glared back at her for a long moment. Finally he said, "Now, get the hell out of here and leave me alone."

Two sharp rings from the doorbell shattered the tense silence of the room.

For a moment Karen stood immobile as though she hadn't heard. Then, slowly, she began to move out into the hall. She paused for a second to pat the back of her hair and check the seams of her stockings.

Just as the bell sounded again, Karen reached the door.

CHAPTER EIGHT

K AREN HAD GIVEN very little thought to the sort of person Miss Proctor might be. Yet, as she opened the door and faced the woman, Karen felt somehow that Miss Proctor had been sent as just punishment for her sins. The woman stood a good six inches taller than Karen, her figure firm and trim inside its uniform, the hands gripping her purse immense and thick knuckled. It was the face, especially the eyes, which frightened her. Hard, unrelenting, nerveless eyes. And Karen knew instinctively that this woman would devastate her home as efficiently as an atomic bomb.

"Mrs. Edgemont?"

The deep, cold voice cut sharply across Karen's nerves and she started self-consciously, realizing that she had been staring at the woman. "Yes, of course," she said. "I'm sorry. Please come in."

Miss Proctor picked up the battered black valise beside her and followed Karen inside. Without turning to look at her, Karen felt the woman examining, evaluating, measuring everything in the apartment.

"Uh ..." Karen heard herself sputtering and stopped short. It was foolish of her to be afraid of this woman. After all, Bill had recommended her highly. He must know what he was talking about.

She tried again. "I've fixed up my husband's den for you. It's right down the hall. Near the bedroom."

She started down the hall with Miss Proctor right behind her. "I hope you'll be comfortable here." She wished the woman would say something.

Miss Proctor set the valise firmly beside the couch. She glanced quickly around the room and nodded. Then she looked directly at Karen. "You've been crying," she said matter-of-factly.

Karen's hands flew guiltily to her cheeks, still flushed and damp from her tears. She must look a sight. A fine impression she must be making on this stranger.

Miss Proctor did something with her face that was probably meant to be a smile. "I didn't mean to startle you," she said. Her tone was hard and monotonous. "Dr. Stacy has told me all about your husband's case." She smiled again. "I'm sure it hasn't been easy for you."

"No. No, it hasn't." Something about the way Miss Proctor looked at her set Karen's teeth on edge. And the way she had said *all* about Steve's case. Had Bill really told her everything? About Steve? About...

Karen dismissed the thought that came to her mind quickly. Bill wouldn't have told anyone about that. He couldn't possibly have done so. Yet she knew that the woman must know of Steve's impotence. And Miss Proctor was hardly the type to sympathize with a woman's need for sexual outlet. She looked as though sex were an experience she had never encountered and wanted no part of.

"As soon as you've gotten settled," Karen said evenly, "I'll introduce you to my husband. He's waiting for us."

"Then by all means, let's go in," Miss Proctor answered. "I'm as settled as I'll ever be."

In spite of the thousand little worries nibbling around the edges of her brain, Karen felt herself beginning to relax about the woman. It might not be such a bad idea to have someone like Miss Proctor around, after all. Certainly Steve needed someone with a little more strength and purpose than she herself had been able to offer him. And perhaps she could even learn something of those qualities from this woman. She could surely use them. Especially now. If she were ever to get anywhere with Steve after this latest episode, she would need all the strength she could muster.

When they entered the bedroom, Steve hunched himself up against the pillows, but made no sign of greeting to either of them. He looked gaunt, inexpressibly tired, his mouth drawn to a thin line of suffering. Karen realized suddenly that he had not seemed this much in pain even immediately after the accident. And she knew the sinking feeling in the pit of her stomach to be guilt. And fear.

Yet she approached the bed with as much outward assurance as though things were ideal between them. "Darling, this is Miss Lila Proctor," she said evenly.

Steve did not even glance at her. Nor at Miss Proctor. He turned his head toward the window and determinedly proceeded to ignore them both.

Karen looked up at Miss Proctor and lifted her shoulders in a gesture of helplessness and apology.

The woman pursed her lips thoughtfully for a moment and frowned a deep furrow between her eyes. Then, very deliberately, she stepped around the end of the bed and into the line of Steve's vision.

She held out her hand. "Mr. Edgemont."

He hesitated, meeting the woman's gaze steadily. Karen watched a pink flush of embarrassment spread over his pallid features. And in her heart she smiled as Steve raised his arm stiffly to shake hands. Obviously, Miss Proctor had met and managed Steve's kind before.

There was no hint of triumph on Miss Proctor's face. As she began to straighten up the rumpled sheets, her movements were crisp and efficient. Steve made no sign of objection to her ministrations.

Yet Karen could see the resentment and suspicion in his eyes as he watched Miss Proctor move about the room. And she knew that he was still condemning her for the woman's presence in their home.

"You didn't finish your lunch," the woman said, tapping the edge of the night table with one blunt fingernail. She glanced accusingly from the untouched tray to Steve's annoyed face.

"I wasn't hungry."

"Well, now. If you expect to get out of that bed ..." She didn't finish the sentence. She simply picked up the tray and started with it toward the door. She nodded to Karen. "If you'll just show me to the kitchen ..."

Karen jumped as though she had been slapped. "Oh, yes. Of course," she murmured feebly. She glanced for a second at Steve, who was glowering after Miss Proctor's broad back, then followed the woman quickly out of the room. "This way," she said.

In the kitchen Miss Proctor immediately acquainted herself with the setup and began pulling neatly wrapped packages out of the well stocked refrigerator.

Karen stood just inside the doorway, watching, wondering what, if anything, she was expected to do. Finally she began to sense a growing discomfort, manifesting in a prickly sensation across her shoulders, an aching low in her back. It was bad enough certainly that she had fought with Steve. Even though their disagreement had been fairly violent, she believed that they would have been able to work everything out satisfactorily between them. As they always had. But she felt, somehow, that Miss Proctor would interfere, that the woman would always get in the way. And suddenly she did not want Miss Proctor to cook for Steve, to feed him and tend to all the duties that were rightly her own.

She took a step forward into the room. "Let me help you," she said. "I don't mind the cooking."

Miss Proctor slid a steak in under the broiler. "It's no trouble," she said over her shoulder. "Besides, I like to take care of everything for my patient. That way, I'm better able to judge the progress he's making."

"I see," Karen murmured. Miss Proctor's tone left no room for disagreement.

"Furthermore," Miss Proctor went on, "your husband will be on a special diet from here on in." She stopped to hold a match under the broiler, then set the oven dial. "We have to build up his strength, you know, now that he'll be getting up soon. Though I think maybe Doctor's hurrying things a bit."

"What do you mean?"

The woman's face grew serious. "He doesn't look at all well to me," she said. "Nervous as a cat. Fretful."

Karen sighed deeply and sat down on a chair next to the table. "It's just today. We..." She paused uncertainly, wondering just how much she dare say.

Miss Proctor didn't wait for her to finish. "I think I understand, Mrs. Edgemont. Apparently your husband doesn't realize that you have had problems, too." She smiled. "Men are like that sometimes."

The monotonous tone of the woman's voice did not so much as waver. Yet Karen felt herself becoming wary, defensive. Maybe it was only her own guilt. Maybe it was all in her own warped imagination. Still, she had the uncomfortable sensation of being baited. She could not understand what Miss Proctor might be trying to do. But, whatever it was, Karen knew that she did not like this woman. Not at all.

She sat watching the woman prepare Steve's dinner. Neither of them made any further attempt at conversation. And Karen was thankful for the moments of quiet. Yet she sat tensely on the edge of her chair, her hands clenched tightly in her lap, as though she expected something dreadful to occur at any moment.

When it was ready, Miss Proctor swung the tray easily off the cupboard and started out of the kitchen.

Karen rose quickly to follow her.

"I think perhaps you'd better wait here," Miss Proctor said crisply. "Since he's already upset…"

If she finished the sentence, Karen didn't hear it. She stood looking after the woman, clenching and unclenching her hands, suffering the indignity of impotent rage. She had had just about enough of Miss Proctor. And the woman hadn't yet even unpacked her bag.

Yet, Karen realized that there was nothing she could do. Absolutely nothing, if she loved Steve. For Miss Proctor had been sent to help him get back on his feet again. And she was obviously very capable at her job. Left alone, she was far better equipped to care for Steve than Karen herself would ever be, no matter how much she loved him.

Even realizing the truth of the situation, Karen felt no sense of relief. Tiredly she stepped to the sink and once more filled it with hot soapy water. Funny, she was beginning to feel like a scullery maid in her own home. All she seemed able to do anymore was mop around the edges of other people's activity. At least there had been some excuse for it as long as Steve had been dependent on her. Now…

What an empty, futile, stupid thing her life had become! First, she had allowed herself to become obsessed by her need for sexual fulfillment. And when she had realized the utter hopelessness of promiscuity, she had resolved to sublimate her needs and devote herself, heart and soul, to helping Steve. And now that even he no longer wanted or needed her … What was she to do?

She worked the scouring pad listlessly inside the frying pan, hardly aware of what she did. She had never felt so completely exhausted, so utterly useless in her life.

Before she had finished at the sink, Miss Proctor returned with Steve's tray.

"I'll take it," Karen said, taking the tray from the woman's hands and sliding the dishes from it into the sink.

"He ate everything," Miss Proctor stated complacently. "I think we'll get along just fine."

Karen glanced away so that Miss Proctor would not see the pain in her eyes. She did not need to be told that Steve responded favorably to everyone but herself. She already knew that. And for an instant she wanted to shout at the woman, tell her to get out of their house and let them alone.

Instead she managed a smile. "I'm certainly glad to hear that," she said. "I'm afraid I haven't been a very good nurse. Perhaps it's because…"

"It takes an impersonal attitude no wife could have," Miss Proctor interrupted. "I'm sure you've done your best. You love your husband."

She said it as a statement of fact, yet Karen heard it as a question and knew that Miss Proctor had meant it that way. Still, she let it pass without comment, not wanting to cause a disturbance. She turned back to the sink and busied herself with the dishes.

"Well, if you'll excuse me… I'd like to unpack."

"What time would you like dinner?" Karen asked half-heartedly, dreading the thought of sitting down to a meal with the woman.

"Oh, don't give it a thought. I'll just take myself a little something. Later on."

Karen listened to the solid thud of the woman's flat heels echo along the hall. She whipped a towel off the rack next to the sink and picked up a dish. Her hands shook so that she could barely hold onto it. She set it into the cupboard, then reached for a cup. It slipped from her fingers and clattered into the sink.

Almost in tears, she flung the towel away from her and ran from the room. In the living room she started toward the couch, wanting to throw herself face downward and sob out the unhappiness, the frustration that had been building up in her all day.

Yet, she realized, she didn't dare. What if Miss Proctor should hear? What if she told Bill? Whatever else happened, Karen knew that she must stay away from Bill now. For the temptation to lose herself in his arms was a challenge she dare not face. Especially now, when everything else in her life appeared so grim.

She went into the bathroom and locked the door behind her. Leaning against the sink, she peered into the medicine cabinet mirror, hardly recognizing the distraught features peering back at her. Hollow-eyed, tense, tearful. A lovely vision. No wonder Steve could barely tolerate the sight of her. She opened the cabinet, took out a bottle of aspirin and swallowed three with a gulp of water. It wouldn't really help, she knew. Nothing could reach the heart of her trouble.

Nothing.

Dropping her things around her as she undressed, Karen stood dismally in the center of the bathroom, examining the bruises Bill had left on the insides of her thighs. Had it been only yesterday? Already her body had forgotten. There was nothing now but the bruises. And the guilt.

She turned on a blast of hot water in the shower and stepped under the spray. She didn't really feel like taking a shower. She had to admit she didn't really feel like doing much of anything. Her life had become an endless round of soap and scrubbing, yet somehow everything remained a sort of muddied gray. Even hope had become a fraud. What was there to hope for, anyhow? Even if Steve recovered, she had no assurance that he would love and want her as he once had. The rift between them gaped dangerously wide and even in her imagination she could see no way of mending it now.

Moving the rough cloth slowly over her body, Karen considered how she might best approach him.

He had every reason, after all, to consider her a slut. And no matter how vehemently she might try to deny his accusations, she could not deny the truth to herself. Still, if he would only give her a chance, she felt positive that she could prove herself worthy of his love. Even his trust. Yes, she had made a mistake. But must that mean the end of everything for them? If they loved each other enough, wouldn't they be able to rise above this thing that had sullied their relationship? She knew it would never happen again. Never.

Even as she vowed to herself that she would not even allow herself to be tempted into a repetition of the episode with Bill, Karen's body screamed in protest. Everywhere she touched with the cloth, the flesh responded eagerly, anxiously, wanting more. And, as the awareness of this seeped into her consciousness, Karen felt herself gradually losing control. She could not for a moment forget her need. Nor could she fulfill it. She felt a sudden thumping ache behind her eyes as the futility of her situation became more obvious to her and for a terrible instant she thought she must surely be going insane.

She turned off the water, but she did not have the strength nor the courage to move.

With her back sliding along the steamy tiles, she sank slowly down to the floor of the shower stall and sat there, huddled in the corner, her knuckles pressed against her mouth.

She became aware finally of the coldness of the tiles creeping into her skin, numbing her. And she pulled herself up and stepped out onto the mat.

Grabbing a fluffy towel, she wrapped it around herself and rubbed briskly, trying to get warm.

Her only hope now lay with Steve. She knew that she must tell him everything that had happened. Tell him and pray that he could forgive her. Perhaps together they would be able to find a way. For she had gone beyond the point where she could rely on herself.

She dressed carefully and applied her make-up with a shaky hand. She hadn't bothered to set her hair for days and she pulled it back now into a chignon, tucking the damp ends in neatly.

All things considered, she felt that she looked rather well.

After a final check in the full-length mirror behind the door, Karen left the bathroom grimly determined to face Steve and have this thing out once and for all.

She thought for a moment that he was asleep, hunched down in the bed with the blanket pulled up tight under his chin. But, as she quietly approached the bed, she saw his eyelids open ever so slightly and knew he watched her every move.

She took a deep breath and with it summoned up every ounce of courage she had left. "Steve …"

"You still here?" he muttered.

"Darling, I … I have to talk to you. About us," she finished weakly. If only he would stop fighting her. Just for a moment.

She heard him sigh, the disgust obvious in his tone.

"Why don't you give up?" he said finally. "Don't you know yet it's over between us?"

"Do you mean that, Steve?"

"I mean that."

"I'm sorry, darling," she said very quietly, so he would not know her misery. She felt as though her heart had leaped into her throat. "I only wanted to tell you …"

"I don't want to hear it."

This time, when he closed his eyes and turned away from her, Karen did not try to draw him back. She felt utterly defeated at last.

She hardly noticed Miss Proctor, hovering in the hall, disapproving. She didn't care about Miss Proctor now. She didn't care about anything, except getting as far away as she could.

She picked up her purse from the table in the living room. Then, without looking back, she fled the apartment, slamming the door behind her.

CHAPTER NINE

S HE WALKED BRISKLY down Fifth Avenue beside Central Park, not heading anywhere in particular, yet too full of anger to stroll. Steve was being positively infantile. Feeling sorry for himself. And maybe he had a right to. But he certainly had no business throwing her out into the street like this without even hearing her side of the story.

Why couldn't he fight back like a man, instead of wallowing in self-pity?

Well, that was his problem now. His and Miss Proctor's. He didn't need a wife anymore. He had made that clear enough, certainly.

Yet, now that he had set her free, what was she supposed to do?

Her thoughts raced furiously and she quickened her pace to keep up with them. Ahead of her the lights of the Fifty Ninth Street circle blinked between swaying branches, beckoning to her with the sweet promise of life. Of excitement. Perhaps she should take a room in a hotel, find herself a job. She could still type well enough to pass a test. Maybe they would be able to have the marriage annulled because of Steve's condition. She would really be free then, to seek a new love, to find the fulfillment she so desperately craved. She would be free ...

And then what? What decent man would want her now? A woman who could not even be faithful to a broken man. A woman with one ruined marriage already on her record.

The realization hit her with blinding force. Indeed, who would want her now? Not even Bill, for all his fine words. He only desired her as a sexual partner, of that she felt sure. And she did not intend to be anyone's mistress.

At Fifty Ninth Street, instead of going to find herself a place to stay, Karen turned into the park and walked down the winding path to the edge of the lake. An early evening breeze ruffled the surface of the water and Karen cupped her elbows in either hand, aware suddenly of the chill and the growing darkness. Aware of the anger burning itself out, subsiding into depression.

For a while she strolled beside the lake, watching couples walking dogs, couples laughing, couples... No one seemed to be alone but she. The sense of isolation only served to increase her depression. Her head still ached and she felt positive that her right heel had blistered. She was miserable and tired. And more than anything in the world, she wanted to stretch out and sleep.

Yet... Where? All the determination she had felt only moments before drained away, leaving her aimless and a little desperate.

She sat down on a bench beside the path and slipped off her right shoe. With her thumb, she explored the tender area and found a watery blister the size of a dime. Whether she liked it or not, she couldn't possibly just continue to walk around all night. She could barely walk now. She put the shoe back on and started to get up.

When she saw him, she thought perhaps he was someone she knew. He came toward her along the path, walking slowly, but obviously headed in her direction. She watched him approach, curiously, wondering what he might want with her. She did not recall having seen him before, yet she felt no nervousness about his presence. It was not yet dark and there were strollers close by, certainly within shouting distance.

Short and stocky with a thick mass of oily black hair, the man was neatly dressed in a black suit and charcoal overcoat. As he stopped a few feet away from her, he hunched the heavy coat forward on his shoulders and jammed his hands into his pockets.

He stood there staring at her, his black eyes almost luminous in the on-coming darkness.

For a moment she waited, expecting him to speak. For some reason she still felt that she must know him from somewhere. He certainly didn't look like the type to accost women in the Park. Yet, as he continued to stare in silence, she felt as though the night had suddenly grown very cold. Long fingers of fear crept up to grasp at her throat and she began to shiver uncontrollably.

She took a deep breath, trying to get a grip on her chattering nerves. "What do you want?" she croaked.

The man said nothing. He didn't even move.

Yet suddenly she knew that she had better get out of there. And fast. She made a movement to rise and grimaced with pain. She couldn't possibly run with that blister. Not even to save her life.

Apparently her movement had been exactly the wrong thing to do. He took several steps toward her, then stopped again.

And now she could see the furtive movements of his hands where the coat bunched between his legs.

Blister or no blister …

She stood up abruptly and started to run across the grass, toward the entrance.

He grabbed her before she had gone twenty paces. As his coat fell away, she saw that he was exposed. He grabbed her by the wrist and pushed her hand hard against him.

Karen's eyes widened in horror. She opened her mouth to scream.

His fist caught her right across the mouth. She felt her teeth cut deep into her lower lip and tasted the salty tang of blood on her tongue. Her senses reeled from the blow and she felt herself slowly begin to fall.

He grabbed her roughly by the arm and shoved her down to her knees.

She fell sideways onto the grass. She felt his fingers tearing at her clothing, shoving at her skirt. The flimsy material of her panties shredded in his hands.

And then he was on top of her, forcing her legs wide with the bulk of himself. She heard his hard, rasping breathing, grunting like an animal. The odor of his sweat mingled with the smell of damp earth in her nostrils.

Then there was nothing but the pain, the hideous pain as he ripped into her brutally. He hacked at her mercilessly with the murderous weapon of himself, grinding her naked buttocks into the damp grass. The pain became almost unbearable, till she felt as though her guts had been torn wide open. Once more she tried to scream. His mouth came down hard on hers, smashing her lips against her teeth, his tongue probing against hers.

All she could think was, I deserve this. Steve would tell me I deserve this.

And she prayed to God to give her the strength to endure.

She heard the breath go out of him explosively and he lay like a dead weight on top of her. She felt herself losing consciousness, the world, the park, the man whirling away from her, tilting crazily like a clown. Her fingers clutched convulsively for something to hold onto. Then everything was quiet and still.

The water lapped languidly against the lake shore. Somewhere on the street a whistle blew shrilly. Yet she lay still for several seconds listening before she remembered where she was and how she came to be there. She sat up then and looked around hastily for her assailant. But he had already disappeared.

Karen dragged herself painfully to her feet, wobbling precariously on her high heels. Forlornly she picked her way back toward the pavement, smoothing her skirt down as best she could. Retrieving her purse from where she had dropped it in the grass, she began to make her way back toward the entrance.

All of her ached as though she had been pummelled by many fists and she limped badly now. She did not know where she was going. She didn't care. Yet she had to get away from the scene of the incident.

Ahead of her she saw a man coming toward her, leading a frilly French poodle on a slender chain.

Insanely she believed him to be the attacker, returning. She began to run across the grass, up the hill. Stumbling. Her heart beating furiously, achingly in her throat. Twice she stumbled and clambered up again.

When she reached the shadowy fringing of trees, Karen knew she could run no more, She collapsed, breathless and sobbing, against the gnarled trunk of a tall oak.

CHAPTER TEN

KAREN DID NOT know how long she huddled there, clinging to the bark of the tree, shivering. Yet she heard the terrified whimper of her own crying and realized she was nearly hysterical with fear. The awareness brought with it a gradual return of steadiness and she found a handkerchief in her purse and dabbed at her eyes.

As she touched her mouth, Karen swallowed hard to keep back the cry of pain. Gently she felt around her swollen lip with her fingertips. It was stiff now and crusty with blood.

My God, she thought. *I must be a sight.*

In the light from a streetlamp she examined as best she could the extent of the damage. Her skirt was torn and streaked with grass stains, her stockings in shreds. Somehow she had lost the heel off her left shoe. And her panties...He must have taken them with him.

She realized that a lady in distress should go immediately to the police. Yet... she wasn't a lady anymore. The police would ask questions, take her home, probably talk to Steve. And Steve would tell them about her, all right. Tell them that she was a whore who picked up any man she could get. Who would believe her story then, when her own husband accused her?

She made her way slowly along the edge of the lawn toward the Fifth Avenue entrance. With a blister on one foot and no heel on the other shoe, the going was tedious.

But obviously she had to go somewhere. In this condition she could hardly wander the streets.

She could go home…

Where is home, Karen? Just where is home?

Bill would be glad to take her in. Glad to see that she had left Steve. But she had already promised herself to stay away from him. The price she would have to pay for his help was more than she was prepared to give.

There was no one left but Jean. The only friend she had now. Yet how could she face the woman in this condition? Only a few hours ago she had been babbling to Jean about becoming the perfect wife. Would Jean believe her story about the man in the park? After all, why should she believe it, when she had seen Karen in a similar predicament just yesterday? All women are inclued to sneer when another woman cries rape.

Still Karen realized that she had very little choice in the matter. As she came out of the park, she turned up town in the direction of an outdoor phone booth she had noticed earlier, afraid to take the chance of walking into a drug store.

She found a dime in her purse and dialled Jean's number. The phone rang six times before she answered. Her voice sounded like she had just gotten out of bed.

"Did I wake you?" Karen asked, concerned that she might be disturbing the woman beyond reason.

"Not at all. I was just… resting."

The peculiar tone in Jean's voice bothered her. Yet Karen had too much on her mind to be rattled now by such a minor thing. "I… I'd like to come up," she blurted. "If you don't mind." She paused. "Something… something's happened and I need your help."

"Proceed at your own risk, honey," Jean cooed through the phone. "I've got half a high on now. And I'll probably be crocked by the time you get here."

Karen sighed with genuine relief. "I can use a little of that myself."

She hung up and stepped to the curb to hail a cab.

The driver looked at her strangely. But he reached back to open the door and helped her inside. She gave him Jean's address, then slumped back against the cushions, welcoming the chance to relax and stretch out her aching limbs.

Karen was relieved that Jean had merely been drinking. For a moment she had thought she might have interrupted Jean with a man. After all, the woman had quite openly admitted being unfaithful to her husband.

Why?

It had never occurred to Karen to wonder what had driven Jean to seek love away from home. Allen was obviously in love with her. Why, then, did she turn to others?

Karen sighed, realizing there was still much she did not understand about the world and its ways. How could she expect to make sense out of Jean's situation when she could make none out of her own?

The cab sped her rapidly toward the Bronx, swerving in and out of the light evening traffic. The driver glanced at her now and then through the rear view mirror. But he made no attempt at conversation and Karen was grateful for his silence.

She tried hard not to think about the incident in the Park. Still, she could not forget her aching limbs nor the cut, swollen lip. It had been foolish of her to walk alone in the park at dusk. She had read enough warnings against it to have known better. Really, she had no one to blame but herself.

Yet she knew in her heart that it was Steve she blamed. Not only for tonight. But for Bill. For her own inability to cope with the sexual situation resulting from his accident. Though she almost hated herself for the thought, she knew that, if he had faced up to the matter like the man she had thought him to be, they would have been able to work something out. Together, the way people in love should do. He had left the whole matter up to her until it had been too late. And now, they must both suffer as a result.

She told herself over and over and over again that it wasn't fair to blame him. That he had too much thrown at him all at once. No one could be expected to respond any differently than Steve had. Yet, no matter how often she said it, there it was. The ugly truth. She had lost faith in him, completely and irrevocably.

And it was high time she began making plans for herself that did not include him.

By the time the cab drew up in front of Jean's house, Karen had worried herself into a state of nervous exhaustion. She knew she would never be able to walk as far as the door on that blistered heel. Carefully she worked the shoe down off her heel. The stocking was damp with blood where the blister had broken open and rubbed. Carrying both shoes, she got out of the cab and started up the walk.

She heard the cabbie whistle a comment through his teeth as he drove off.

Jean was waiting with the door open by the time Karen reached the porch. As she saw her friend's dishevelled condition in the glow of the porch light, Jean stepped forward to lend a hand.

Karen sagged limply against Jean's arm.

"I guess you meant it," Jean murmured. She led Karen inside and closed the door. "Something happened."

"I thought you were drunk," Karen said, trying to offset the impression of her appearance. "You said on the phone…"

"Forget what I said on the phone. What happened, Karen?"

Karen lowered herself stiffly onto the foam rubber couch and sat carefully erect on the edge of it. "I asked first," she pouted.

Jean burst out laughing, then came over to her quickly as Karen's face puckered with confusion. She sat down beside Karen and put a hand on either side of the girl's face.

"Forgive me," Jean said gently. "It's just that you looked so funny, darling." She peered closely at the bruised lip. "I know it must hurt terribly."

Karen felt as though the flesh under Jean's hands had burst suddenly into flame. There was something infinitely gentle, almost caressing about the way Jean touched her now. Something about the way she smiled into Karen's eyes that touched a responsive chord deep inside Karen and made her uneasy. She knew that she was flushed with embarrassment, yet she could do nothing to control the unexpected reaction.

"I'm all right now." She tried to keep her tone light. "Really I am."

Jean shook her head disbelievingly. "You look pretty battered to me, honey. But I won't ask any questions, if that's what you want."

"All I want is to stretch out and relax for a few moments," Karen sighed.

"No sooner said…" Jean stood up beside the couch, then stooped to swing Karen's legs up onto the pillows. "There. Now, you just take it easy and I'll bring some ice for that lip."

Karen sighed again, feeling intensely weary. "It might do me more good if you put that ice in a glass and pour a little Scotch over it."

Jean hesitated, then shrugged amiably. "Anything you say, honey. But I hope you know what you're doing."

"I know all right," Karen murmured.

She watched Jean move off toward the kitchen. She was glad now that she had come here. The woman's easy charm, the cozy, comfortable room did much to ease her troubled spirit. She knew without asking that Jean would let her stay the night. And in the morning, perhaps she would see about finding a job and a place to live.

But there would be plenty of time to think about that later. All she wanted at the moment was to forget. Forget everything, all the ugly, sordid details of the past few days. And in Jean's company, she felt that she would be able to do so.

Jean came back into the room carrying a hammered silver tray. She set the tray on the coffee table and uncorked the bottle of Scotch. "Say when," she smiled.

When the tumbler was half full and Karen still had not told her to stop, Jean lowered the bottle and set it back on the tray. "I told you once before, this is not the way." She handed Karen the glass, then sat into the sling chair across from the couch. She had taken nothing for herself. "All that will get you is a hangover and a guilty conscience."

For a moment Karen studied the ice floating in her glass. "I've tried everything else," she said. "Nothing else seems to work either." She tilted the glass to her mouth, but did not drink, letting the ice cube rest against her swollen lip.

Jean took a cigarette from the pack lying open on the coffee table and tapped it against her thumbnail. "Maybe you've overlooked a thing or two," she said, very quietly, looking not at Karen, but at the cigarette. "After all, you're not the only one around with problems."

"I suppose you've solved all yours," Karen snapped impatiently. She couldn't bear it when Jean spoke to her that way, as though she were an inexperienced child. If Jean could only know what she had been through in the past few days, she wouldn't be sitting there so piously. Jean probably wouldn't be speaking with her at all. But then, she couldn't possibly know. Her husband was still in one piece.

Jean smiled, but only with her lips. Her eyes showed a suffering that rose from deep inside. "No. I haven't solved mine, Karen. But at least I try."

"I'm sorry," Karen blurted, embarrassed by her own clumsiness. "I keep forgetting…"

"It's all right," Jean said quickly. "I shouldn't have said anything." She laid the cigarette, still unlit, onto the coffee table. "Look, drink that stuff and we'll get you into bed. You've probably caught your death of cold as it is."

Karen sensed that Jean was deliberately steering away from the subject, yet she could not understand why this should be so. The woman had been eager enough to talk the last time they had been together. Apparently something she had said just now had upset Jean. Yet what could it have been?

She sat up on the edge of the couch, resting the moist bottom of the glass in one palm. "I didn't mean to hurt your feelings," she said. "It's just... Well, you must realize that my situation isn't quite so simple as yours, Jean. After all, Steve has been very badly hurt. It's been a month already and we don't know when he might be fully recovered. Things haven't gone very well between us. I mean, we haven't..." She felt as though the words had stuck fast in her throat. She tried to say it, but nothing more would come out. Hastily, she gulped down a swallow of her drink.

"What you mean, I presume, is that he can't make love to you anymore," Jean said simply.

"Yes," Karen nodded.

"I wish I could say the same."

"What?" Karen was sure that she couldn't have heard Jean correctly. Yet she felt a peculiar twinge of excitement begin to stir along her spine.

Jean shook her head and abruptly stood up. "Don't pay attention to me, little one," she murmured. "I'm no one to give you advice."

"No. Wait," Karen insisted. "I want to know what you mean."

"And maybe someday I'll tell you. But right now, it's time for good little children to get some sleep."

Karen finished the Scotch and set the glass down on the tray. She felt distinctly uncomfortable now, yet she could not quite put a finger on the source of her discomfort. "Jean," she said, a worried frown etching deep into her forehead, "you don't love Allen, do you?"

Jean started to laugh, but quickly got control of herself. She put on an expression to match Karen's. "No," she said quite seriously. "I don't love Allen. I never have."

"But, I don't understand. Why..."

"I won't try to explain," Jean said. "We do many things that don't make sense, Karen, even to ourselves. I married Allen because he loved me and I needed to be loved. He's away a good deal of the time, racing at one place or another, so we manage." She shrugged. "It's not very satisfying, but it's a kind of security."

Karen frowned uncertainly. "But you said there have been others, Jean. What if you find a man you love?"

Jean grinned and reached to pat Karen's cheeks with the tips of her fingers. "Don't worry about that," she said. "There's not a chance in the world." She held out her hand. "Come on. Now."

Without another word, Karen let Jean lead her out of the room and down the hall. A thousand questions popped about in her brain. But she remained silent, suddenly uncertain and a little afraid of this strange friend.

CHAPTER ELEVEN

A<small>FTER A LONG</small> soak in a hot tub, Karen began to feel almost human again. Her back and shoulders still ached, her thighs were a mass of ugly, livid bruises. But the warmth of the water, the Scotch she had drunk earlier combined to soothe her jangling nerves, lulling her with the promise of peace and rest. The hideous episode with the man in the park had already become a vague image, not to be forgotten, but to be thought about later when she could cope with it better.

Standing on the fluffy yellow bathmat, leisurely patting herself dry, Karen listened for sounds of Jean moving about the house. She hoped that Jean would have gotten over her peculiar mood by now and that she would not insist on going to sleep right away. For there were many things Karen needed to get straightened out about her future. She didn't expect Jean to be able to help. But the least she could do would be to hear her out.

She pulled on the flowered flannelette nightgown Jean had left for her, then slipped into the soft pink robe. The material felt smooth and good against her flesh and she stretched languidly, enjoying for the moment the sensuous thrill of it. She had begun almost to hate her body or the senseless demands it made on her, driving her headlong to her own destruction. Yet now she felt utterly relaxed, calm, in control of herself and her emotions. And she believed herself capable of handling any challenge life might present her with.

Anxious to share these feelings with her friend, anxious to get down to this business of living, Karen flung open the bathroom door and stepped out into the hall.

"Jean?" She waited a moment and, getting no answer, called again. "Jean, where are you?"

Footsteps hurried toward her from the back of the house. "I'm right here," Jean said easily. "I was just talking to Annette on the phone. She called to invite herself over for a drink."

"Oh," Karen sighed, the disappointment plain in her tone. She remembered clearly the tension Annette's presence had caused the last time the three of them had been together. And tonight she needed to talk quietly with Jean. Alone.

Jean smiled at Karen's response. "Don't worry," she said. "I told her not to come. I didn't think you were in any mood for company."

"I didn't mean to ..."

"Don't give it a thought. I can see Annette any time. But you ..." She didn't finish the statement, but cupped Karen's chin in one hand and tilted her face to the light. "How's that lip?"

"Practically healed. In fact, I feel wonderful."

Jean frowned at her dubiously, her green eyes dark with concern.

"No, really. I mean it," she insisted. "A couple of hours ago, I thought the end of the world had come. And now ..." She shrugged. "I'm ready for anything."

Jean leaned back against the wall and folded her arms across her stomach. Her tanned face above a arms man-tailored blouse looked flushed and a little worried. "You'd better get to bed anyhow," she said seriously. "You've had a pretty rough day. Judging from appearances. And I don't want you passing out on me."

Karen felt a happy laugh bubbling up inside her. She couldn't explain why, but she was beginning to be lightheaded, almost giddy. And the worried frown on Jean's face looked so out of keeping with her own mood. Jean should be smiling. Relaxed.

"It can't be the alcohol," Jean said. "You didn't have enough."

"It's just me," Karen laughed. She felt so cheerful she couldn't bear to have her friend be unhappy. "Don't you see? I've been so worried about…about everything. And now, none of it seems important anymore."

Solemnly Jean shook her head. "No, I don't see," she said, her tone still serious. "All I can see is that you're being half hysterical and telling me you're fine. I don't think it's funny at all." She sighed and stood away from the wall. "Still, I don't suppose there's much I can do about it, is there?"

Karen just smiled.

"Come on, then. We'll have coffee and you can tell me all about yourself."

Obediently Karen followed her friend along the hallway to the kitchen. She had never seen Jean in slacks before and she glanced now admiringly at the trim figure outlined dramatically in black. If she had a figure like that, maybe Steve wouldn't have become so indifferent. Oh, her body wasn't all that bad, but she certainly couldn't wear anything that tight with her hips. Jean had a flat, firm behind and almost no hips at all. The kind of figure women dieted to own.

In the kitchen she stood just inside the door, watching Jean bustle about fixing the coffee. She felt much too excited to sit calmly by while someone else was being active. She moved across to the stained oak cupboard and pulled open a door.

"I'll do that," Jean said quickly, as she reached for a cup. "You just take it easy tonight."

Lifting out cups and saucers, Karen carried them to the table and set them down. Then she went back to look for the napkins.

Jean shook her head scoldingly, but not disapprovingly. "What are you trying to prove, honey? You don't have to pretend with me."

Karen stared at her in pretended wide-eyed innocence. "But, Jean, I'm not trying to prove anything," she said seriously. "I mean it. Everything's worked itself out clearly in my mind. The things that have been bothering me are no longer problems. And

I know exactly what I'm going to do with my future. So ..." She raised her shoulders.

"Let's go sit in the living room." Jean lifted the heavy pot onto a tray and set the cups and saucers beside it. "At least let me sit down and be comfortable, if we're going to be serious."

Karen enjoyed having Jean pamper her like this. She knew she would have welcomed attention from anyone just now. But there was something special in the quality of Jean's friendship that comforted her. She let the woman sit her down on the couch and pour her a cup of coffee. Balancing the cup carefully, she curled up against the pillows and pulled her legs up under her.

Jean took a cup for herself and crossed to the sling chair. "Well, let's hear it," she said. "Whatever it is you're so excited about." Gracefully she lowered herself into the awkward seat.

Karen detected a hint of amusement in Jean's tone and glanced quickly at the woman's face. Yet she could find nothing there except a friendly interest. She took a sip of the strong black brew and lowered her cup to the table.

"Well, I haven't really told you what happened," she began. "So I suppose we'd better start there." She paused. Then, looking directly into Jean's eyes, she said, "Steve and I are through."

"Oh?" Jean's eyes twinkled with disbelief.

"Finished. For good," Karen said firmly.

"Uh huh," Jean murmured. 'And it seems to me that just this morning you had decided to be forever faithful and true." She raised an eyebrow skeptically. "Is it possible that you're just a little bit confused, my dear?"

Karen smiled. "I deserve that," she admitted. "I have been carrying on like a fool. But things have changed since this morning. You see ..."

"He threw you out," Jean said flatly.

Karen was startled by the accuracy of Jean's guess. She watched her friend's eyes closely. "Yes, he did. But what difference does that make now?"

Jean sighed tiredly. "None. Now. But it will," she said with the same tone of authority. "The irate husband usually storms out of the house in a fit, Karen. Steve couldn't very well do that, so he threw you out instead."

"And?"

"He always comes creeping back, my friend. And, because you feel guilty, you'll decide that you really love him after all, no matter what's happened between you. You'll go back, Karen. Take it from me."

"But that's just the point, Jean." She heard the tremor in her own voice. "I don't love him. I couldn't possible love him and feel the way I do now."

Jean gave a short, hard laugh and, hearing it, Karen felt her own light spirits beginning to wane. It seemed preposterous to her that Jean should doubt her sincerity, when she was herself so fully convinced of her feelings. Yet, knowing Jean's doubt, her own convictions no longer appeared quite so sound. Perhaps she had simply failed to communicate all that she felt. Or perhaps Jean had an insight she herself did not have, based on experience that was truly valid.

She put her forehead against the back of the couch and hugged herself tightly together. "You make me sound pretty foolish," she murmured.

She heard Jean pull herself up out of the chair. And then the woman was sitting beside her on the couch. Not touching her quite, but very close.

"Karen, listen to me for a minute, will you?" Jean said quietly. "Nothing would make me happier, believe me, than to think that you really had decided what you want. But I know that's not possible, honey. It's not all that easy. You haven't stopped loving Steve just because he can't satisfy you sexually anymore." She touched Karen's arm gently with her fingertips. "And stop blushing."

"I'm sorry," Karen whispered, still blushing, but unable to control it. There was something almost frightening about being so transparent. It seemed that Jean could see into her very heart.

"But it's always convenient," Jean went on, "to have a good excuse for being unfaithful. Most of us try to rationalize away our sins. And if you could manage to convince yourself that you really don't love him, then you could do anything you wanted to do without feeling guilty. But you're lying to yourself, child. And I just hope I can make you realize that before it's too late."

Karen felt herself beginning to relax and a smile tugged encouragingly at the corners of her mouth. She had listened to every word. Carefully. But something about Jean's little speech did not ring true.

She turned slightly against the pillows, but kept her glance averted. "Aren't you the one who was encouraging me just the other day to accept this business as being natural? Didn't you say I shouldn't feel guilty?"

Jean smiled ruefully. "That was the other day," she said calmly. "I've changed my mind."

"But, why?" Karen asked. "I'm still the same person I was then." She could make no sense out of any of this, she realized. And her head was beginning to whirl with confusion. She had counted on Jean to help her, to strengthen her own convictions. Yet Jean had denied everything that Karen herself believed.

She faced Jean squarely, her unhappiness and confusion etched clearly in her expression. "I don't understand what you're trying to tell me," she said pitifully.

Jean looked at her for a long moment. Then, suddenly, she got up and stepped away from the couch.

Karen frowned, more confused now than ever. For a moment she believed that she must have offended Jean to have made her jump away like that. She seemed to be offending people all the time lately.

Yet, when Jean turned to face her, her features were soft with emotion. Her voice, as she spoke now, was gentle and kind. "Karen, I had no right to tell you the things I did," she said. "I suppose that I wanted to believe that you were like me. Like Annette. But I realize now that I was mistaken. You love your husband. That's pretty obvious. You don't think so at the moment, I know. But that's only because you're unhappy and confused."

Her voice lowered and her eyes clouded with an emotion Karen could not interpret. "I've never loved my husband. I've never loved any man. I've told you that. And that's the difference between us, honey. It's as simple as that." She shook her head. "The rules I live by just won't work for you."

Karen leaned forward to the table and raised the cup to her lips, needing something suddenly to hide behind. Despite the kindliness in Jean's tone, she felt that a rift had been made in their relationship. Jean no longer considered her a real friend, no longer trusted her as she once had. And Karen knew she could not afford to let this happen. She needed Jean's friendship now.

For, whether Jean accepted the fact or not, Karen knew that she would never return to Steve. Her future was a question to which she still had no answers. But she would need Jean's friendship, her help.

"I'm not sure I understand everything you've said," Karen stated quietly. "And I don't want to argue about it anymore tonight. I'm much too upset to think clearly."

"Of course," Jean said. "That's why I wanted to pack you off to bed as soon as you got out of the tub. No one could be expected to think clearly enough to make decisions in the state you're in."

Karen sighed and pushed herself up from the couch. "All right. I give up," she conceded. "Maybe in the morning, when I'm rested ..."

Jean nodded with satisfaction. "That's better," she said. "I've got the bed turned down, all ready for you. All you have to do is hop in."

Karen hesitated. She had no right to keep pestering Jean. Yet she knew she would not be able to sleep now. Not alone. "What about you?"

"Oh, I won't be sleepy for hours yet," Jean said easily. "After all, I haven't had as much excitement today as you've had."

"Well…" Karen murmured indecisively.

Jean stepped toward her briskly and cupped one hand under Karen's elbow. "You're worse than a two year old."

Karen let herself be steered into the bedroom and she had to admit to herself that the big double bed looked inviting. She hadn't slept in a real bed since the night before Steve's accident.

And she had forgotten how truly exhausted she was. Yet now, sitting on the edge of the firm mattress, she knew it would be good to stretch out and rest.

Jean took the robe from her and draped it over the back of a straight chair against the wall. She stood with her fingers on the light switch as Karen climbed in and snuggled down under the covers.

"Good night," Karen said in a little girl voice.

Jean smiled warmly. "Good night."

And then the room was plunged into darkness.

She heard Jean pull the door closed behind her and walk softly back to the living room. The whole house seemed enveloped in silence and there was something almost sinister about the darkness and the silence. She lay immobile in the center of the bed, breathing deeply, listening for the sound of her own breathing. It sounded large in the stillness and she shivered under the warm blankets, afraid and wanting to call to Jean to put on the lights.

You're acting like a fool, she told herself. *There's nothing to be afraid of here. It's just nerves.*

Scolding herself didn't help anything. It was always like this in the dark lately. Fear, reaching out to strangle her. Fear, paralyzing her mind, torturing her body.

Yet what was she afraid of now? Before, it had been the terrible uncertainty. Her days had been empty, her nights filled with lewd dreams. The dreams had given her an awareness of a need she had tried to deny. Well, there was no need to deny it any longer. If Steve didn't want her, others would. Many others. And she would give herself gladly, oh, so willingly, to anyone who asked. Anyone. Steve had no right to behave as though everything that had happened were her fault. And she would prove, even to Jean, that she could get along just beautifully without him.

Smugly content with her own conclusion, Karen gradually let herself relax, stretching her limbs comfortably and drifting into a hazy half sleep.

In her sleep it was Springtime and she walked alone in a forest of rustling leaves and sweet, new grass. She walked slowly, leisurely, enjoying the beauty of the scene. There was a lake in the distance and, when she spied it, she wanted to hurry toward it, to plunge into its cool depths.

She began to run. Faster, faster. But suddenly she was limping, as though a pebble had gotten into her shoe. She heard something behind her and, turning, she saw him. That man. Wearing an overcoat of charcoal gray. Coming toward her. She slipped on the grass and fell headlong. He was bending over her, tearing at her clothing. The coat fell open.

She screamed.

She felt someone shaking her, calling her name.

She screamed again.

"Karen. Baby, wake up. Look at me."

Dimly she heard Jean's voice, felt Jean's arms go around her. She knew then that she was safe and she let go the tension inside her. Her body shook with sobs.

Jean sat beside her on the bed, cuddling her close like a frightened child. "Go ahead, honey," she crooned. "Get it all out. All of it."

Karen felt Jean's fingers stroking her hair, soothing her. She nestled her face against the woman's neck, trying to stop the flow of tears, yet not wanting to give up the comfort of Jean's attention.

Finally she took a tissue from the woman and dabbed at her eyes.

"Better?" Jean murmured.

She tried to answer, but could only sniffle and gasp out a hoarse sound.

Jean laughed and sat Karen up straight, holding herself at arms' length. "Now, that's more like it," she said, crooking a finger under Karen's chin. "You're almost smiling."

Despite herself, Karen did smile, a little lopsidely, but gratefully nevertheless. "I'll be all right," she managed. "Just a dream. A nightmare."

Jean nodded. "I didn't reaize just how upset you were or I wouldn't have left you alone."

"I didn't either," Karen admitted. "I thought I had put it out of my mind." She glanced up at Jean cautiously. "Maybe I'd better have another drink. So I can sleep."

"Oh, no you don't," Jean said firmly. "You have to live with yourself sometime, baby. You might just as well begin right now."

"Please."

Jean stood up and switched on the bedside lamp. "There," she said. "That'll do just as well. I'll stay with you until you fall asleep."

"But I won't be able to sleep," Karen insisted. "I know myself too well."

Jean sighed. "All right. But this is the last time." She went out of the room quickly and returned in a few moments carrying a tumbler half full of Scotch.

Karen took the glass and eagerly gulped down the contents. The whiskey hit her stomach like a balled fist. She felt her senses reeling and shook her head sharply to regain her equilibrium.

She had forgotten that she had not eaten all day. And now the liquid burned through her, fuzzing her brain.

Jean set the glass on the night table. "I'll be right back," she said. "Try to sleep. She switched off the lamp and left the room.

Alone again in the dark, Karen had a sudden, senseless urge to giggle. She felt very proud of herself for the way she had managed Jean.

And the alcohol had been just exactly what she needed. So what if she couldn't think straight? There wasn't anything she wanted to think about anyhow. And the delicious numbness spreading through her limbs, easing her body would waft her right to sleep.

Yet even now she felt the vague stirring of the one sensation she most wanted to stifle. The familiar aching in the pit of her stomach, the tightening muscles of her thighs. Uneasily she realized that the alcohol had merely rekindled the flame of her desire.

She turned onto her stomach and buried her face in the pillow. She must not let Jean know.

When Jean came back into the room, she did not turn on the light, but crossed directly to the bed. Karen felt the mattress dip as the woman got in beside her.

Jean stayed far over on her side of the bed.

Karen groped in the darkness toward the lamp.

"What's that for?" Jean frowned at the light. "I thought you were asleep."

"I was looking for you," Karen said innocently. "You're so far away, I didn't know you'd gotten into bed."

Jean raised an eyebrow. "Oh?"

Karen patted the mattress beside her.

"You're drunk," Jean said flatly.

Karen giggled. "Do you hate me?"

"It would be a lot easier if I did," Jean murmured.

"What?"

"Turn off the light."

"Not till you move over here," Karen insisted. "I'm lonesome." She hardly realized what she was saying. Yet she wanted Jean to be close to her, close enough to touch. She wanted Jean to hold her again, the way she had a few moments before. Maybe then the aching need would quiet. Maybe then she would be able to sleep.

Jean moved two inches nearer.

"Here," Karen said.

Propping herself on one elbow, Jean leaned across her and snapped off the light. Before she could lie down again Karen slipped an arm around the woman's waist and held her fast.

"You don't know what you're doing," Jean whispered.

Karen felt the woman's body warm against her own. Indeed, she didn't know what she was doing. She didn't even care. She knew only that her flesh burned with the need to be caressed, to be loved.

Her hand moved to caress Jean's back.

She heard Jean suck in her breath. And then the woman's mouth was touching her own, gently, searchingly.

She pulled Jean hard against her, forgetting her swollen lip and bruised body, remembering only the demands of her love-starved body.

And suddenly Jean was no longer resisting her. Her hands, her lips played Karen's body with sure knowledge, her tongue probing and finding the tender, intimate areas of her flesh.

Karen abandoned herself willingly to the waves of sensation rolling through her, arousing her to a shuddering pinnacle of desire. She felt Jean's lips moving downward, burning a path of promise. Jean's cheek, soft against her thigh.

"Do it. Oh, do it," she murmured.

And then the world fell away from under her as she arced like a rocket through space, to explode in a thousand shimmering points of light.

She lay still for a long time afterward, cradling Jean in her arms, gazing past the woman's shoulder to the moonlight seeping in through the window. She could not be sure yet just how she felt about Jean. But of one thing she was positive: She had been as completely satisfied by Jean as she had been by any man.

CHAPTER TWELVE

WHEN KAREN AWOKE, Jean had already left the room.

Stretching luxuriously in the big bed, Karen sensed an unfamiliar lightness and suppleness in her limbs and body that she knew had to do with more than a good night's sleep. Gradually she pieced together in her mind the events of the previous evening.

As she recalled that second drink and what had followed as a result, Karen felt herself blushing furiously all over. How could she ever explain to Jean, make her realize that she had never done such a thing before? That the demands of her body had stifled all inhibitions?

And yet, she hadn't done anything, really, except touch the woman. It had been Jean who had understood. Jean who had known what to do to satisfy her need. And remembering what had happened between them, Karen realized that the woman obviously knew very well what she was about.

Suddenly many things became clear in Karen's mind. She understood now why Jean felt as she did about men, about the man she had married. Understood, too, Annette's hostility. Annette must have been jealous. And if that were true, it could only mean that Jean had been attracted to her for some time.

Karen wasn't entirely sure she liked the thought that followed next. Yet it seemed logical enough. After all, she had enjoyed the experience with Jean thoroughly. And she had been completely satisfied.

Surely that must mean ...

"Hi, there," Jean said cheerily.

Karen had not heard her come in and she started guilty, as though Jean might have sensed her thoughts. But the woman's calm expression erased all misgivings.

Karen smiled warmly as Jean set a cup of coffee on the night table. "What time is it?" she asked. "I feel like I've slept forever."

"Almost noon." Jean stepped back from the bed and folded her arms. Her blonde hair had been pulled into a chignon low on her neck and she looked pink-cheeked and freshly scrubbed. "I patched up your skirt and had your shoe mended. So you're almost as good as new."

Uneasily Karen sensed that Jean was carefully avoiding the subject that, at the moment, interested her the most. Quickly she tried to recall something she might have done to alienate the woman. Yet she felt that Jean's hesitancy arose from somewhere outside herself. Perhaps Jean regretted their intimacy.

Or perhaps she had been disappointed.

"Jean," Karen said carefully, "I...I want to explain to you about last night."

"You don't have to," Jean answered. "I just hope you'll be able to forget it."

"Forget it?"

Jean nodded. "It was my fault. I shouldn't have let you have that drink."

"But..."

"I can't honestly say I'm sorry, Karen. I only hope you'll be able to forgive me someday."

"Forgive you?" Karen wailed. "But, Jean. You don't understand. I wanted you to. I really did. I think I must have been wanting you to for a long time."

Jean sat down on the edge of the bed and took Karen's hands between her own. "Honey, listen to me for a minute, will you?" Her tone was intensely serious. "I know what you're thinking about yourself right now, but it just isn't so. I told you yesterday that you're not like me. You're a perfectly normal, healthy woman, my dear. Yes, you've gotten yourself into a lousy predicament as a result of Steve's accident. And, yes, I satisfied you last night." She grinned. "But I can tell you that's no compliment to me. You've been so tied up in knots that way, anyone would have served the purpose, my dear.

"So don't get any screwy ideas about yourself, little one. You didn't want me last night. I just happened to be handy."

Jean spoke so gently that Karen could not resent her words. Yet she was not prepared to agree with the woman either. Surely she had responded to Jean last night, not just to a physical need. It was foolish of Jean to deny this.

Unless she were merely protecting herself. Unless she were afraid. But of what?

"Jean, I want you to tell me the truth," Karen said quietly. "How do you feel about me?"

Jean averted her glance immediately, but she did not let go of Karen's hands. "That's not what we were discussing."

"That's what we're discussing now," Karen answered. "I want to know, Jean."

Jean shrugged. "I can't see that it makes any difference. You're the one we've got to get straightened out."

"That's just what I'm trying to do."

Slowly Jean raised Karen's hand to her lips and touched it lightly with a kiss. "I'm in love with you, little one," she murmured. "I have been, I think, since the first time I saw you."

Karen let her breath go in a long, contented sigh.

Jean glanced at her questioningly. "What's that supposed to mean?"

"That's known as a sigh of relief," Karen said lightly. "And may I point out to you, now that you've confessed, that you haven't even kissed me good morning?"

She felt Jean stiffen and draw still further away from her. The woman's eyes were moist with pain.

"Jean, what's wrong? Darling, what is it? What have I done?"

"Don't play games with me, Karen," Jean said hoarsely. "I know you can't possibly understand how I feel about you. I don't expect you to. But please, please don't make fun of me, baby."

Never had Karen felt more sincerely about anyone than she did about Jean at that moment. Yet the woman's hesitancy was obviously based on bitter experiences in the past. And she did not know how to tell Jean how sure she was of her own desires.

Very gently she leaned toward the woman and reached out to touch her hair, her cheek. "I could never make fun of you, Jean, without making fun of me, too."

For a long moment they searched deeply into each other's eyes.

And then Jean's arms went around her, holding her tight, pushing her back against the pillows. Jean's tongue teased her earlobe, the hollow of her throat.

She heard herself whispering, "I want you, I want you."

And then she heard nothing, felt nothing but the thumping pulse of her desire. Goading her mercilessly, demandingly. Torturing them both in the bittersweet moment of fulfillment.

Jean rolled away from her and lay on her back, her eyes open, staring blankly at the ceiling.

Karen propped herself on one elbow and peered down curiously into the sad, beautiful face. With the tip of one finger, she traced the outline of a smile around the woman's lips.

"Was it all that terrible, darling?" Karen teased.

The green eyes brought her into focus. "You know better than that. It's just…"

"Just what?"

"I'll be so sorry to see you go."

Karen felt she must definitely have lost her sense of humor if this was meant to be funny. Surely Jean couldn't be serious. If this hadn't proved to her…

"You will, you know," Jean went on.

"How can you say that, after …"

"I've made love to many women, my dear," Jean said easily. "And believe me, honey, your heart's not in it. All you want is to be satisfied." She shook her head sadly. "God knows, I can't condemn you for that. But when a person is truly in love," she finished very quietly, "he knows that it is more blessed to give than to receive."

Karen felt herself flushing hotly. Yet she could not very well deny the truth of Jean's words. Twice she had let Jean make love to her, abandoning herself wildly to the pleasure the woman gave her. Yet neither time had it occurred to her that Jean's need must be as intense as her own. And in her heart she had to admit the validity of Jean's assertion.

"Don't look so desolate," Jean chided. "I'm not blaming you. I'm a big girl. I should know better by now."

"Jean …" Karen moaned desperately.

Jean sat up quickly and kissed the tip of Karen's nose. "Don't listen to me, honey. Sometimes I get carried away by the sound of my own voice."

Karen heard the tinge of bitterness underlining the woman's words. Yet somehow she sensed that Jean felt not so much sorry for herself as just sorry. She could not bear to have Jean blame herself for the failure of this thing between them. But, before she could say another word, Jean got up and started toward the door.

"I'll bring your things," she called back.

Then she was gone.

Karen sat on the bed looking after her, wanting to call her back, yet realizing that she could not honestly say the words the woman needed to hear. She knew that she could never love Jean the way Jean loved her. Real love implied a dimension that no woman could fulfill for her. A home and children, marriage and a life in the community. Even Jean, despite her desires, must know and accept this. Hadn't she married Allen and settled down here, turning a conventional face to the world outside?

Slowly Karen crawled out of bed and began lifting the night-gown off over her head. A half-formed scheme played around the edge of her mind. If Jean were willing, there was no reason she could see why they couldn't continue this relationship. She would be more than happy to give as well as receive. For, so long as her sexual demands were fulfilled, Karen knew she would be able to unravel the tangled skein of her life. Begin to function again like a normal human being.

If Jean were willing...

"You'd better put something on."

Startled, Karen whirled to face her. Jean stood in the door-way, very deliberately keeping her glance from Karen's naked body. The mended skirt hung draped over her arm.

Impishly Karen drew one shoulder back, jutting her breasts forward and up. She watched the pink creep into Jean's cheeks.

"What for?" she teased.

"Because if you don't," Jean said quietly, dropping the skirt onto a chair as she came forward, "we're going to wind up back in bed." She stepped in close to Karen, her palms sliding under the heavy breasts. "And that wouldn't do at all..." She bent her head quickly and darted her tongue into the still moist cleavage. "... because I've got breakfast on the stove."

Karen laughed easily and kissed the woman on the lips. "In that case, go and let me get dressed."

Humming happily to herself, Karen slipped into her cloth-ing and borrowed one of Jean's combs to smooth out her hair. Suddenly her life had become remarkably uncomplicated, all her confusions settling comfortably under the assurance that, with Jean's love and help, she would be able to solve everything. All she had to do now was decide what she wanted to do with her future. And together, they would make it come true.

For with Jean, Karen had found what she had been seeking all her life. Jean wanted her. Unconditionally. And it was to this Karen responded as much as to the woman herself.

If only Steve had been able to love her that way!

She cut the thought off abruptly and hurried out to the kitchen. As she entered, Jean turned toward her, the telephone receiver clutched tightly in her hand.

"It's for you," Jean said, her voice unsteady.

Karen took the receiver slowly, almost unwillingly, not wanting to hear the voice on the other end of the phone. For she knew even before she spoke that the neat little dream she had planned for herself with Jean had already been destroyed. Destroyed beyond all hope.

"Hello…" she breathed. "Yes, yes. Of course I'm all right…"

She listened to Bill's voice explaining to her that he had found her address book and been calling every name on the list in the hope of finding her. He spoke very precisely, as though preparing her for a shock that might prove too much for her to bear.

Yet when he told her what had happened, she was not even surprised. Somehow she had known…

Woodenly she handed Jean the receiver. Somewhere inside her a tremor of fear stirred.

"What happened?" Jean asked quietly.

"Steve," she whispered. "He tried to get out of bed. To come find me and bring me home." She felt the sting of tears behind her eyelids. "Bill says… He… he hurt himself pretty badly."

"And he wants you," Jean said calmly.

Karen glanced at the woman quickly, sensing the sarcasm behind her words. "Yes. He… Oh, Jean, he wants me to come back."

"Well," Jean sighed. "that's that. I didn't think it would be quite so soon, but maybe it's better this way." She paused. "For both of us."

"Oh, Jean, please don't say it that way. I don't know…"

"You're going back, aren't you?"

"I have to, Jean. He needs me."

"Maybe you mean that you need him," Jean said, her tone steady.

Karen stared at her, unable to answer the accusation in the woman's words. Even a few moments ago, she had been positive that Steve was out of her life for good. And now...

Now she could barely wait to reach his side.

"Come on," Jean said, putting her arm around Karen's shoulder. "I'll drive you."

CHAPTER THIRTEEN

A<small>LL THE WAY</small> back into Manhattan, Karen kept trying to convince herself that everything was going to be all right. After all, Bill had told her on the phone that there was nothing to worry about. Yet she had sensed something in his tone that belied the bland assurance of his words. And she felt the icy hand of fear reach out now to clutch at her heart.

She left Jean in front of the apartment house with a promise to call her as soon as she could and hurried across the pavement to the canopied entrance. She was grateful that Jean had taken everything so well. And she knew that, no matter what happened now, Jean would always remain her friend. Still, she could not help but feel that she had not been fair with Jean. She had offered herself to Jean. Offered herself, then withdrawn.

Quickly she pushed the thought out of her conscious mind and hurried down the hall to their apartment, fumbling in her bag for the key. As she reached the door, it swung wide to greet her. She hesitated on the threshold.

Bill looked her over slowly, critically, his glance settling finally on the still swollen lower lip. "I'm glad you decided to come," he said finally. "I'd like to talk to you, Karen. About Steve."

She walked past him, down the foyer and into the living room. She heard the door close quietly and his footsteps coming up behind her. Nervously she pushed a strand of hair off her forehead.

Bill touched her arm lightly and tried to peer into her eyes.

She saw the deep lines of concern etched across his brow and quickly averted her glance. She did not want him to see her guilt, her confusion. "Please don't lecture me, Bill," she murmured. "Even if I deserve it."

He stepped away, then turned to face her. "I wasn't about to," he said evenly. "I know what happened here yesterday. Miss Proctor told me the whole story. And, believe me, the only reason I bothered to call ..." He shrugged. "Well, you've told me that you love him. And I knew that you'd never forgive yourself if ..."

"That's true," she interrupted quickly. She took a step toward the hall. "I'd better go in to him."

"There's no hurry," Bill said. "I've given him a sedative. He'll sleep for hours yet."

Sighing tiredly, Karen let herself down into the softness of a huge armchair. "How is he, Bill? Really."

His lips tightened thoughtfully. "That's pretty difficult to answer," he said slowly. "Physically, I can't say that he's actually worse than he was before. But mentally, things look pretty grim."

"How do you mean?"

"Oh, I suppose that I mean that Steve's given up the fight." He shoved his hands into his pockets and strolled away to the window. "As a doctor, I've done everything I can for his body. Yet somehow I feel that I haven't really helped him at all. He isn't responding to treatment because, apparently, he no longer cares."

Karen nodded dismally, understanding all too well what Bill meant. Hadn't she felt the same way yesterday, when she knew that their marriage was ended?

"It's my fault," she said simply. "I had no business leaving him, no matter what happened between us."

He turned and leaned back against the sill, looking at her now directly. "Perhaps," he said. "But no one in your position would have done otherwise." For a moment his glance dropped and he seemed absorbed in the nails of his right hand. "It doesn't matter at this point what either of you should or should not have done, Karen. What you've got to decide is what you intend to do now."

"Why, help him, of course. In any way I can," she said impatiently. "What would you expect me to do?"

"First of all," he said evenly, "I would expect you to take time to think this thing through. You've got to be honest with yourself, Karen." He looked at her levelly. "If you come back to him now and then, for any reason at all, decide to leave him again, I'm not sure that he would be able to recover. Before you see him, you must decide what you want, Karen. And this is no time to be noble."

She stared at him blankly, unable to comprehend why he should be talking to her in this way. He knew perfectly well, after all, that she was still in love with Steve. Of course she would stay with him. Stay with him forever, no matter what might happen.

"I don't understand what you're trying to say, Bill. I'm so muddled in my own head, maybe I just can't think straight. But I can't see any reason..."

"Karen, be reasonable, will you?" He pushed himself away from the windowsill and came to stand over her. "You didn't love Steve any the less a couple of days ago. Yet you came to me in a state of complete nervous exhaustion. The situation hasn't changed. If anything, it's even worse. It's extremely unlikely that Steve will ever again be a man in the sense that you need him to be, Karen." He paused and his expression became even more serious. "If you couldn't cope with that fact a few days ago, there is no reason to assume that you will be able to do so in the future."

She felt herself beginning to tighten up inside, her nerves and her fears responding spontaneously to his words. It sickened her to believe that she might be so shallow. That her life and her love could revolve around the fulfillment of her sexual needs.

Yet everything Bill had said was true. Perhaps it always would be true.

"I don't know," she murmured finally. "I just don't know."

"I do," Bill said firmly. "You're a completely normal, healthy human being, my friend. You're not the type to devote yourself to nursing an invalid." He leaned close and peered earnestly into her eyes. "You've got to think of yourself."

"That's exactly what I have been doing," she said bitterly, "thinking of myself. And, considering the results, I'd better start thinking about someone else for a change." She met his glance defiantly. "Or would that be inconvenient for you, Dr. Stacy?"

"This has nothing to do with me, Karen," he answered blandly. He looked deliberately at her sore mouth. "Obviously you do quite well elsewhere."

"Oh, you make me sick," she blurted. She flung herself out of the chair and away from him, the accusation in his tone. What right did he have to criticize and condemn her? Yet she knew it was not Bill she despised, but herself.

She took a few faltering steps, then paused helplessly. Feeling the sting of tears behind her eyelids, she buried her face in her hands.

Almost instantly he was beside her, his arm going around her shoulder to pull her close.

She leaned her forehead against his chest and closed her eyes.

Somehow, Karen realized, she always wound up like this, in the wrong person's arms. Deriving strength and courage from casual embraces she had no right to know. Yet she needed Bill now to hold her. To hold her and to want her. And deep within her she felt the stir of desire. A desire that knew no limits and could find no satisfaction. A desire that was slowly driving her out of her mind.

She moved in closer, insinuating herself against him, her fingers trailing up the back of his neck, along the hairline.

Instantly his arms dropped to his sides and he stepped away from her.

She peered up at him curiously.

"You don't know whether you're coming or going, do you?" His brow furrowed with concern and she could see the professional attitude take over in his manner. "It wasn't three minutes ago that you were ready to devote the rest of your life to an impotent man."

She jumped back as though he had slapped her. She knew she was flushed and shaking. He had spoken gently, yet every word had hit its mark like a steel tipped arrow. Ashamed, confused, she lowered her glance.

He was quiet for a long time. She could almost hear his doctor's brain, weighing, evaluating her behavior.

"I think you need help, Karen," he said finally, his voice low, kind.

She could have laughed in his face. "Then help me," she almost screamed.

"I'm not sure that I can anymore."

"What am I supposed to do?"

He looked at her steadily for a long moment before he answered. Then he tilted his head slightly to one side. "I think perhaps you'd better consult a psychoanalyst," he said quietly. "I can recommend an excellent one."

For an instant she wanted to slap his handsome, serious face. Then, abruptly, she laughed.

"You find it amusing?" he said crisply.

"I find you amusing," she retorted. "Haven't you just been telling me how healthy and normal I am."

He let his breath go in a long, tired sigh. "All right, Karen. But I hope you'll heed my advice before it's too late. Even you must be aware that your behavior has become, shall we say, a bit erratic. You can't be happy like this."

Suddenly Karen knew that she had to get away from him. Instantly. She hated Bill now as she had never hated anything in her life. Not for himself, not even for the things he had said to her. But for seeing too much of the ugly truth about her.

For knowing things about her she had not even dared admit to herself.

Very calmly, she faced him, forcing herself to smile a little. "Have you said all you had to say, Dr. Stacy?" She did not give him a chance to answer. "If so, I think you'd better leave now. I'm sure Miss Proctor will be able to take care of the patient."

One eyebrow rose even so slightly. "Oh?" he said. "And what about you?"

She smiled again, coldly. "I'm quite capable of taking care of myself, thank you."

He shrugged and turned toward the door. "In that case…"

Stopping just long enough to pick up the little black bag, he was gone almost before she realized it. She heard the door slam, the clang of the elevator down the hall. Still she stood looking after him dumbly, unable to muster the strength to move.

A psychoanalyst? He must really think she was already pretty far gone. Oh, she knew that he hadn't meant to imply that she was insane. Everyone went to analysts nowadays. She had heard someone say that analysis had replaced baseball as the national sport. Still, as far as she was concerned, that remained strictly a luxury, designed for those who hadn't the courage to face their problems. Or their responsibilities.

And Karen felt far from ready to admit defeat.

Filled now with a new sense of determination, Karen ran quickly through a mental list of things that had to be done, if she were going to be living with Steve again. First off, she would have to make peace with that ogre, Miss Proctor. For without the woman's cooperation, she would be unable to get even close to Steve, do the intimate things for him that he used to like to have her do.

She had no illusions that it would be a simple matter to get back into Steve's favor. His dismissal had been scathing and complete. Pride would keep him from going back on his words now. Yet she believed that, deep in his heart, Steve still loved and wanted her. And as long as she could go on believing that, Karen knew she still had a chance.

It would take time. Maybe a lot of time. But what they had once had between them had been perfect. And she longed to recapture the essence of their early love.

And having Steve's love would solve everything.

Except…

For a moment a sad smile touched the corners of Karen's lips. Jean. What must she do about Jean?

Whatever else she might do about the woman, Karen knew that she would have to be sincere. Honest. For Jean's sake, as well as her own and Steve's.

But this was no time for thinking about her past mistakes. It was a time for courage. For action. She pulled herself up straight and inhaled deeply.

Then she started quietly down the hall toward the bedroom.

Miss Proctor's uniformed figure loomed in the study doorway. "You'd best not go in just now," she said. "Doctor wants him to sleep as long as possible." She eyed Karen critically, scarcely bothering to conceal her opinion of the battered features.

"Yes, I know," Karen said, ignoring as best she could the woman's frank appraisal. "Actually, it was you I was looking for." She managed a wooden smile. "I thought perhaps we could discuss my husband's condition."

She watched an expression play across the woman's eyes that looked suspiciously like a smirk.

If she had thought to curry the woman's favor by seeking her confidence, Karen realized that she had made a grave mistake. Obviously Miss Proctor had reached her own conclusions about Karen's interest in Steve's condition. And just as obviously, Miss Proctor was secretly delighted at Karen's misfortune. Karen had known instinctively that the woman did not like her. Yet now she felt completely baffled, unable to comprehend any explanation for the woman's open hostility.

"What is it you'd like to know?" Miss Proctor said blandly. "I heard you speaking with Doctor. I thought…" She raised one hand in a gesture meant to finish the sentence.

Karen felt her cheeks go hot. Just how much had the woman actually heard?

"Yes, yes," she said quickly. "I simply meant…" Oh, what the hell did she mean, anyway? Words spun incoherently across her mind. She felt the pulse begin to throb in her right temple.

Miss Proctor waited patiently for her to go on.

"Well, I thought that, since he needs day and night care now, we might be able to divide up the work. I mean…" She felt her tongue tripping over her own confusion. Rather than blunder foolishly on, she shut her mouth and glanced pleadingly at the other woman.

"That's perfectly all right, Mrs. Edgemont," Miss Proctor said, her tone almost patronizing. "I'm used to difficult cases. I think I'm capable of managing."

"I didn't mean…"

The woman smiled benevolently at her distress. "What did you mean?"

Karen could have spit in the ugly, evil face.

Instead, she smiled in return. "I'm sure you can manage," she said calmly. She turned half away from the woman. "I'm sorry to have troubled you."

"No trouble at all."

Karen heard the study door close firmly behind her. Points of irritation jabbed along her spine. She wanted to slam open that door and heave the creature into the street.

Yet what could she do, even now? Steve needed the woman's trained care, needed the woman now more than he did his own wife.

She glanced toward his door. It was closed tight. She sighed tiredly and turned back toward the living room.

Well, she thought, that failed beautifully. What do I do now?

What, indeed, is a wife to do with herself when she has become completely unnecessary?

She strolled to the wide window overlooking the Park and watched the hazy shades of evening creep up past the trees. She realized vaguely that this had become the only spot in the apartment where she still felt at home. Most of her hours here were spent in front of this window, gazing wistfully out across the Park, watching the sun yo-yo over the trees. And she glanced down now to the carpet beneath her feet, feeling foolishly that by now she must have worn a hole through to the floor.

She could not bear the beaten, futile image of herself. She spun away from the window and searched anxiously about the big room for something to do, something to become involved with. For three seconds her glance clung to the cover of a magazine she'd bought and never opened. But that, too, was futile. She couldn't possibly read. Not now.

The liquor cabinet seemed to beckon.

She knew she'd feel better if she took a drink. Just a little one.

She strode quickly toward the cabinet, determined, if not to drown her troubles, at least to ease them.

She already had the bottle in her hand when she remembered what had happened the last time she took a drink. What would happen if she took one now. Even a very little one. First, the soothing warmth, spreading easily through her, relaxing her. Dulling her perceptions, quickening her pulse.

And then, the other sensations, the stirring of desire, the persistent urging of her physical self, driving her, demanding fulfillment.

Karen stared for a moment at the bottle clutched in her hand. The hand trembled, the palm felt slippery with perspiration. Her head throbbed.

With jerky motions, she set the bottle back into the cabinet and slammed the door. Slowly she rubbed her palms down over the curve of her hips.

Was there to be no escape for her? Ever?

Hardly realizing what she did, Karen pushed one foot after the other, needing the safety of motion to regain her shattered equilibrium. As she walked, a thousand jagged realizations cut across her consciousness, forcing her finally to face up to the reality of her situation. The reality and the hopelessness.

It had been foolish of her even for a moment to believe that she might come back here and start out fresh. She knew that now. No matter how much she might desire it for herself, she could not alter the blunt, ugly set of circumstances that faced her.

Whether she liked the situation or not, the fact remained that her sexual needs were strong and a vital part of her being. Even now, just thinking about it, she sensed the heaviness of frustration dragging at her limbs. That part of her was something that would never change, couldn't possibly change.

And Steve...

She felt the sting of tears behind her eyes. Her nails dug deep into her palms. She loved him, she really did.

And because she loved him, the best possible thing she could do for him was just to get out of his life altogether. Now, before he woke up. He need never know she had returned at all. And, in time, he would forget her.

The more she paced and the more she thought about it, the more positive Karen became that her choice was the only sensible one. After all, hadn't Bill himself told her that Steve might never recover if she stayed with him for a while, then left again?

But where could she go this time?

She didn't want to be alone, to think...and remember. And she certainly had no right to go back to Jean.

Unless...

She grabbed at the half-formed thought and clung to it as though for life itself.

Now that she would be able to prove to Jean that she had left Steve permanently, perhaps Jean would be able to accept her.

122

And her love. Oh, Karen knew that it would take her time to forget Steve, time to work out the many problems of her life. And she knew that she would not be able to do this alone.

Still, she believed, if Jean could only be patient with her, just give her the time she needed... Together they would be able to work out something very fine for themselves.

Without stopping to consider all the implications of her decision, Karen hurried to the phone and dialled.

Jean was delighted to hear from her and listened attentively as Karen poured out her thoughts in a hasty burst of words. Then, to Karen's surprise, instead of inviting her to come up to the house in the Bronx, Jean asked Karen to meet her downstairs in front of the house in an hour.

Puzzled and frowning, Karen turned from the telephone and nearly collided with the starched front of Miss Proctor's uniform.

"Oh, I'm sorry," she said quickly, grabbing hold of the edge of the telephone table to steady herself. "I didn't hear you come in."

Miss Proctor nodded stiffly. "Just going to get myself a bite of supper," she said. "You'll be going out again?"

Karen was determined this time not to let the woman get the better of her. She met the accusing eyes levelly.

"Yes, I'll be going out again," she said. "For good this time, I'm sure you'll be happy to know."

She watched a faint tinge of pink spread across the woman's cheeks. And, for the first time since she had met Miss Proctor, Karen felt a sensation of satisfaction.

"If you don't mind," she went on as casually as she could, "you can tell Dr. Stacy that I've taken his advice." She smiled. "I'm sure you know what I mean."

The woman's nostrils flared ever so slightly, but she made no attempt to refute the statement.

Instead, she simply nodded again and took a step toward the kitchen.

"Just a moment," Karen said sharply, her voice steady now and commanding.

Miss Proctor paused, but did not turn to look at her.

Karen ignored the woman's rudeness. "I'd rather my husband didn't know I've been here," she said, her tone quite serious now. "I ... It might upset him."

This time it was Miss Proctor's turn to smile. She turned to face Karen squarely, pale lips drawn taut across wide, blunt teeth. "You needn't worry about that," she said. "I had no intention of telling him." Karen watched the woman go on out to the kitchen. For one second she was furious, wanting to go after the woman and slap that foolish grin off her face.

Then she shrugged. Miss Proctor was no longer her problem.

Nor, for that matter, was Steve.

Yet, when she heard the tinkle of the little silver bell, she felt her heart convulse in a sudden, terrible spasm.

Miss Proctor's rubber soles squished across the kitchen linoleum. She burst through the doorway almost on the run. As she hurried past Karen, she kept her glance squarely ahead, trained on the closed door at the far end of the hall.

Karen listened and heard the door close quietly. Then the low mumble of Steve's voice.

She could not make out the words.

She did not move until Miss Proctor emerged from the room carrying a heavy tray.

Then she started forward tentatively, wanting to know, yet almost afraid to ask. Finally she mumbled, "You ... you didn't tell him I'm here?"

Miss Proctor hardly glanced at her. "He didn't ask."

CHAPTER FOURTEEN

KAREN HUDDLED DISMALLY inside the doorway, watching for Jean's station wagon.

Inside the light Spring coat she had grabbed as she fled the apartment for the last time, her body felt cold and numb. For a few moments the doorman had tried to make conversation with her. Then, getting no response, he had gone on about his business. From time to time she sensed him glancing at her curiously and then she would look up and try to smile. After a half dozen times, she stopped pretending and sank back into her melancholy thoughts.

Again she had not bothered to pack any of her personal belongings. She didn't care. There was nothing in that apartment she wanted, nothing that would not remind her constantly that she had failed. Failed not only as a wife, but as a woman as well. Surely no mature adult had ever gotten herself so completely fouled up. Other women ...

Just what did other women do, Karen wondered, when faced with a similar situation.

Bill had told her than many men were impotent, for one reason or another. Surely their wives must suffer some of what she had gone through. How did they handle the problem?

Of course, things would have turned out differently for her if she had known her husband's love for more than the short three months of their marriage. Or if they had only had a child. No woman could feel complete without children.

Karen became so engrossed with her ruminating that she did not even notice the station wagon when it finally drew up to the curb.

Jean leaned across the front seat and pushed open the door for her.

The doorman cleared his throat. "Excuse me, ma'am."

Startled by the sound of his voice, Karen caught her breath sharply and glanced toward him.

He nodded in the direction of the curb.

Karen thanked him and nearly ran to the station wagon and the promised safety afforded by Jean's presence.

The doorman slammed the door behind her.

Without a word of greeting, Jean drew the vehicle away from the curb and into the stream of traffic. She kept her eyes straight ahead, her expression pleasant enough, but completely impersonal.

For a moment Karen watched the lovely face, waiting expectantly for a smile, some slight sign of recognition. Anything, to help quiet the jangling tumult of her nerves. Jean must know how upset she was, must have sensed it in her voice on the phone.

And if Jean loved her at all, as she claimed she did...

Finally Karen could bear it no longer. "You certainly don't seem very happy to see me," she blurted. "I'm almost sorry I called."

Jean glanced at her briefly, but her expression did not alter. "Why did you?" she asked quietly.

"What?" She stared unbelievingly at the stern profile. "But I...I told you on the phone," she said desperately. "I realized that I couldn't honestly stay with Steve any longer. So..."

"So you decided to give me a turn in this little game you're playing," Jean finished smoothly. "You know, watching you in action is like watching a tennis match. And I can't seem to keep up with the ball."

Karen felt the breath go out of her. She had no idea what might have happened to change Jean's attitude since she had spoken with her on the phone. Yet the woman beside her seemed almost a stranger now.

They turned west at Seventy Ninth Street and sped across Central Park.

Karen wondered vaguely where Jean might be taking her. But she was much too involved with the woman's unfair accusation to question her. Nor could she find words to express the sense of loss and deception she felt. She had put her trust in Jean, relied on her for help. And now...

She glanced out the window beside her, far off at the city lights twinkling above the tree tops. The park lay peaceful and sleeping around them. Her thoughts returned for a moment to the ugly episode by the pond, a scant twenty blocks away. And crazily she considered that the man in the overcoat had probably a more sensible attitude toward this whole business of sex than she had. After all, he promised nothing, expected nothing—just took his pleasure and disappeared. If only she could learn that, could learn not to complicate the sexual act with ideas of love and expectations of loyalty.

If only she could harden herself to the facts of life as other people seemed to live it.

The station wagon stopped for a light.

She felt Jean watching her and turned to meet her glance. The deep green eyes met hers levelly, yet Karen sensed a great unhappiness emanating from their depths. For a long moment they gazed at each other. Then, as the light changed, Jean turned her attention once more to the road.

"Well, why don't you say something?" Jean asked. "Though I think I know what's going on in your head."

Karen smiled to herself, knowing that Jean could not possibly realize what she had been thinking. She hadn't even told Jean of the incident. She didn't want to tell her now.

Instead she said simply, "You have to admit things are a little different from last night."

She watched the laugh lines spring into play around the woman's eyes. Almost imperceptibly, she let herself relax against the leather upholstery. Maybe things weren't going to be so difficult after all. As long as Jean kept her sense of humor, Karen felt that she still had a chance.

Yet as they swung onto the West Side Highway, headed downtown, Karen realized that things were turning out to be far more complicated than she had expected. They couldn't possibly be going to the Bronx. Yet where could Jean be taking her?

"Where are we going?" she asked after a few moments, when Jean had offered no explanation.

"For a drive."

"Oh. I thought we'd be going to your place," Karen said, trying to keep the disappointment out of her tone. She needed to be close to the woman, really close. And not just sitting beside her in a car.

Jean did not look at her. "We can't," she said.

"Oh?"

"Allen's there," Jean said. "He came in this afternoon. Unexpectedly."

Karen felt a flutter in her stomach that she recognized as pure panic. How could everything in her world be so completely mixed up, all at the same time? Still, she could hardly blame Jean for Allen's behavior.

She waited silently for Jean to go on.

Jean fished in the purse beside her for a cigarette. "I wasn't expecting him for at least a month yet. You remember, I told you that. But something happened to his race car that put him out of the competition. And …" She shrugged and brought the dashboard lighter to her cigarette. "When you called, I told him I had to go out for a while." She smiled. "He thinks you're my Aunt Pam in Queens, with a sprained ankle."

Karen sighed. "I feel like I have a sprained head at the moment," she said tiredly. "What on earth am I going to do?"

"Don't sound so tragic, little one," Jean chided. "It can't be all that bad."

Karen tried to smile. "Oh, yes it can," she said. "And worse. I hadn't even bothered to consider what I might do if you couldn't help me."

"Well, we'll find you a hotel room for tonight," Jean said. "That's easy enough. Later on, we'll get you an apartment. And I guess eventually you'll be finding yourself a job. If you're really serious this time."

Karen listened to Jean ramble on, describing accurately the life Karen had pictured for herself yesterday when Steve had ordered her out of his life forever. Hearing it now, spoken by another, Karen began to appreciate the essential lie of the whole scheme. For in her heart she knew that this was not what she wanted for herself, that it never had been.

And even the fact that Jean spoke of helping her, of spending time with her, did little to relieve the growing apprehension.

"I'll be able to get away fairly often to be with you," Jean went on. "I've never been much of a homebody, so Allen is used to not seeing much of me."

They moved through the toll gate and onto the Belt Parkway. Karen glanced idly at the cars moving beside them. Cars containing couples young and old, happy and not so happy, but living normal, old-fashioned married lives. Somehow there seemed to be no relationship between the words pouring from Jean and these simple, uncomplicated people.

And it was toward their simplicity that Karen yearned now, rather than toward the promise of stolen bliss in the arms of the woman.

Still, she was deeply fond of Jean and grateful to her now for the help she offered. She did not want to hurt or offend her. Ever.

She remembered Jean's coolness toward her when she had first gotten into the car. "It all sounds wonderful," she said. Then she added cautiously, "But are you sure you want to...I mean, you didn't seem all this enthusiastic a little while ago."

Jean flicked ashes into the dashboard tray. "I'm sorry about that," she said. "It had nothing to do with you. I've had a bad afternoon."

"Oh?"

"Mmm," Jean muttered. "I always do when Allen gets home from a trip. He thinks he's the world's champion stud." She paused for a moment. "Do you know what it's like to be made love to by someone you don't want?"

Karen flushed hotly. "You should be grateful you have a husband who can," she blurted.

Instantly she felt sorry for the angry words. She twisted her hands together in her lap.

Jean glanced at her and one eyebrow climbed slowly. "Oh?" she murmured. "I'll be more than happy to switch any time you say, little one."

"You know I didn't mean that," Karen said dismally. "I know how you feel about men."

Jean laughed. "I'm more interested that you know how I feel about women."

They turned off the highway into a parking area overlooking the Narrows. The salty odor of fish and water wafted through the open windows.

Halting the car, Jean flicked her cigarette into the darkness and turned in the seat to face Karen Except for a battered convertible some fifty yards away, they were alone.

Karen leaned back and inhaled deeply, savoring the tangy air. "It's beautiful here," she breathed.

For a moment they listened to the lap-lapping of ripples against the rocks. Somewhere in the distance a gull screamed.

Off shore, lights blinked on and off aboard freighters anchored for the night.

"I like it," Jean said.

"Do you drive here often?"

"Yes." Jean was silent for a moment. "Whenever I have a problem to work out."

Karen heard the sadness in the woman's tone and turned to peer at her through the darkness. But she could not make out the expression on the woman's face.

"Have you got a problem now?" she asked carefully.

"Yes," Jean said lightly. "You."

"What makes you so sure?"

Jean did not answer for a long time. Finally, she inhaled a deep breath and began to speak slowly. "You know, it's funny," she said, "but when I left you at the house this morning, I honestly believed that I would never see you again. Except socially, perhaps."

Karen did not like the sound of Jean's words. She started to interrupt. "But, Jean ..."

"Let me finish," Jean said quickly. "I didn't much like the idea at the time," she went on, "but, well ... I knew I'd live through it. I always do, somehow. Still, I almost hoped you wouldn't come back, Karen. For the simple reason that I know I couldn't possibly hold you, little one. No woman ever could."

Karen remained silent. For once in her life, she could think of absolutely nothing to say.

How could she deny such an obvious truth?

"I see you agree with me," Jean said lightly. "Well, that's all right, too. Because ..." She was silent again for a moment. "Well, since I know I won't be able to hold you, I'm willing to settle for just being with you for as long as I can be. On any terms you want it, honey."

There was a certain urgency about the woman's tone that seemed to reach out to Karen, arousing in her sparks of tenderness and warmth. No one had ever felt like this about her before. No one. It was what she had always dreamed of. Had hoped she had found with Steve.

And suddenly she wanted Jean to take her in her arms, to hold her and be tender. Not just as a lover, but as one who truly loves.

Very carefully, she leaned toward Jean, putting out her hand in the darkness to find the woman's hand and hold it. "Oh, please hold me," she whispered. "Hold me."

Jean moved toward her, her arms going around Karen and pulling her close. She drew Karen's head against her shoulder and kissed her gently on the forehead. "Take it easy," she said. "Not here."

But already Karen felt the quivering of desire snake through her. She did not want to wait. She wanted Jean to love her now.

She put her hand behind Jean's neck and forced Jean's face down to meet her now.

For one second Jean held herself back. Then her lips met Karen's hungrily, her tongue darting, probing. Her fingers searched eagerly beneath Karen's coat, found buttons and tore them free.

She felt the warm hand against her flesh, the fingers moving now inside her bra. The nipple hardened at Jean's touch, throbbing with a need of its own.

She forgot that Jean was a woman, forgot everything but the desire swelling, seething inside her, demanding release.

She lay back against the seat and pulled at her skirt.

Jean's warm hand slithered along the inside of her thigh, teasing, fondling.

Karen shifted uncomfortably on the narrow seat, needing to feel, to really feel every touch, every sensation.

Jean's fingers tugged at the elastic of her panties. Karen raised her hips to ease the process.

"Oh, baby, I love you so," Jean whispered close to her ear.

Jean's mouth came down heavily on hers. She met Jean's tongue with her own.

Karen spread her legs wide as Jean touched her.

Swells of sensation rolled through her. She drew her breath in sharply, sucking hard at Jean's mouth, her tongue, surrendering herself completely.

And then the world, the night, the woman spun away from her. She floated calmly, serenely in the abyss of completion.

Jean stirred and sat up, rubbing an elbow with the other hand. "Are you all right?"

Karen smiled contentedly. "Um hmm. I'm fine."

"And I have a broken elbow," Jean laughed. "Next time, let's try a bed." She paused. "If there is a next time."

Karen rearranged her skirt and sat up into the corner of the seat. "You're the hardest person to convince."

"True," Jean agreed readily. "But, then, I have a theory going about you."

"What theory?"

"The one that says you'd be as happy with a chimpanzee if you thought he liked you."

Too stunned by this statement to retort, Karen merely stared at the woman.

"That was a pretty rough way to put it," Jean admitted. "All I meant was, that there comes a time when selfishness ceases to be a virtue." She laughed. "Which probably sounds even worse to you, but someday you'll know what I mean."

Karen's ears burned furiously and a tight ball of anger seemed to be choking her. Yet what Jean was accusing her of was no different from Bill's accusations, or Steve's, or even Miss Proctor's. Everyone seemed to have her all figured out, all right. And she hated every damned one of them.

Why couldn't they understand? Why couldn't they see that she had tried? She really had. In her place, would any of them have behaved differently?

"I think we'd better go," she said when she had regained a little control of herself. "It's late. I still have to find a place to stay."

"I get your message," Jean said easily. "And I guess you're entitled to hate me, if you want to. But, Karen..."

"Yes."

"I do love you, you know. Otherwise I wouldn't bother." She moved her hand to the wheel. "Someday you'll know what I mean by that, too."

Silently, they started back toward the city.

CHAPTER FIFTEEN

A LL THE WAY back into Manhattan, Karen kept repeating to herself the words that Jean had flung at her. And more than once, Karen had to bite her lip to keep from making an angry retort.

Selfishness ceases to be a virtue, indeed. Jean must herself be an expert on the subject of selfishness by now. After all, the woman's treatment of her husband was certainly an indication of irresponsibility. How dare she accuse anyone else of selfishness?

It occurred to Karen that the other people in her life weren't much better than Jean. Steve, even though he certainly had plenty of reason to be interested in himself since the accident. Still, she truly believed that if Steve had only been able to see her side of the situation, their marriage might have been saved. His injuries, his impotence had loomed in his mind as being only a huge injustice to himself. Never for a moment had he really considered her needs.

And Bill? What could possibly be more selfish than Bill's approach to the situation? Taking advantage of Steve's indisposition to force his attentions on his patient's wife. And he had dared to claim he loved her. Just as Jean had claimed to do. And even Steve.

She watched the skyline of lower Manhattan loom large before them as the station wagon emerged from the Battery Tunnel. In a few moments she would have to ask Jean to drop her somewhere.

But where? Midtown, into the noise and the lights and the confusion? She could find a hotel room there easily enough. And once she had a room ...

What then?

Suddenly she knew that she could not bear to be alone tonight. There were too many things she did not want to think about. Too many memories that would come flooding back in the lonely hours of early morning.

Yet she had no friends, now that this rift had come between herself and Jean. There was no one except her mother. Only for a second did she consider going home to Mother. She was not yet ready to make the explanations her parents would demand from her.

"Where shall I drop you?" Jean asked, cutting into her thoughts.

The voice was pleasant enough, almost too pleasant, Karen thought, after what they had just been through.

Yet, what should she expect from Jean? From anyone? She had let herself get involved and whatever happened from now on would be up to her to determine.

Without hesitation, Karen answered, "You can drop me at Forty Second Street." She kept her voice impersonal. "I'm sure I can manage all right from there."

Jean glanced at her curiously, but refrained from comment. She turned off the Highway and drove crosstown toward Times Square.

After awhile she asked, "Do you have enough money?"

"Yes, plenty," Karen said. "Though I probably won't need any."

"Oh?"

Karen heard the concern in Jean's tone and looked at her quickly, not quite sure how best to respond. Ever since she had met Jean, she had been puzzled by the woman's behavior. Joking one moment, bitter and sarcastic the next. There seemed to be no consistency about her moods. For one instant Karen sensed something of the deep well of unhappiness behind the serene, golden features.

And in that instant she understood, too, that Jean did indeed love her.

"I only meant," Karen said softly, all the hurt and disappointment gone now from her voice, "that I expect to be staying with … with a friend. At least until I find an apartment. But tonight…"

"I understand how it is," Jean said. "You've probably stirred up a lot of things in your mind that you're not yet ready to cope with."

Karen nodded. "And I want you to know…" she began, her voice mellow with affection.

"Please don't say it, Karen," Jean interrupted. "You don't have to, you know."

"But I mean it."

Jean looked at her levelly for an instant. "I believe you do," she murmured.

At the corner of Forty Second Street and Broadway, Jean drew to the curb. "Will this do it?"

"Just fine," Karen smiled.

Jean leaned across her to open the door. "I guess this is goodbye."

"No," Karen said sincerely. "Just so long for a while." Impulsively she leaned forward and kissed the woman quickly on the lips. "I'll call you."

She got out and stood watching as the station wagon veered into traffic. She saw Jean glance up to the rear view mirror, then wiggle her fingers in a final farewell.

As soon as the station wagon had disappeared from sight, Karen turned and searched down the street for an empty cab.

A brisk breeze had blown up, bringing with it the promise of rain. Yellowed bits of newspaper eddied in the gutter at her feet.

She pulled the coat more tightly about her and waited as a cab came up to the curb.

She stepped inside and gave the driver Bill's address on East Fifty Fifth Street.

As the taxi moved eastward, Karen relaxed against the red leather seat and closed her eyes. A faint smile played about her lips.

She knew that she could expect neither loyalty nor affection from Bill Stacy. He had already shown her the kind of man he really was. A real bastard, out to take everything he wanted and prepared to give exactly nothing in return.

And if that was the way he liked to play the game, then she would show him that she was a worthy opponent.

Yet, even as she outlined in her mind the plan of attack she intended to use on Bill, Karen sensed that she was neither satisfied nor pleased by the whole idea. Something inside her warned that she had moved too hastily and not at all wisely.

She drew a small gold compact out of her purse and quickly refurbished her make-up, smearing an extra thick coat of lipstick around her mouth and dabbing with a downy puff at the dark circles beneath her eyes. If she were going to play the role of a prostitute, she might as well start looking like one. She examined the garish effect in the tiny mirror. Her features looked pinched and tired, as though she had roamed sleepless through many nights. Well, there wasn't much she could do about that, she decided.

And, after all, Bill was in no position to be fussy.

Karen had never before been in Bill's new apartment. Yet she knew instinctively what to expect. Deep leather chairs, cracked and polished to a mellow glow by many years' wear. Soft pile rugs, a rack of pipes, the stench of tobacco mingling with the ever-present antiseptic air Bill carried with him.

As she rang the bell and waited for the answering buzzer, Karen tried to calculate just how well Bill's practice must be doing to warrant a six room bachelor apartment in such an exclusive building. Whatever his failings as a man, as a doctor Bill had obviously proved himself competent.

She pushed open the door and crossed to the waiting elevator. Its gentle hum and well-oiled movement soothed the ruffled edges of her nerves.

As the door slid back, she pulled her chin up high and stepped bravely forth into the hall.

Bill was waiting in the doorway of his apartment, one hand still holding an open book. She saw one eyebrow crook ever so slightly as he examined her face.

She tried hard to smile pleasantly at him, yet she knew by his expression that the attempt had not been convincing.

He stepped aside to let her pass, then followed her into the large, cozy room.

Without waiting for an invitation, Karen dropped gratefully onto the sofa, glad for the hugeness and solidity of the piece.

For now that she was here, face to face with him, Karen was not at all sure of her motives in coming here. What had she intended to say to him? All the words she had ever known seemed to be spinning across her brain, colliding with each other, bouncing away. Refusing to settle into a single, simple coherent statement.

She glanced up to Bill and found him watching her curiously, obviously expecting an explanation of some sort to come from her.

She raised her hands helplessly. "You were right after all," she said. "I ... I couldn't face up to it, Bill. And ..."

"And here you are," he finished. He seemed to have understood everything from the few words she had spoken. "Would you like a drink?"

Karen hesitated, remembering the bout she had gone through earlier about taking a drink. Yet certainly her fears were out of place here. In view of her intentions, any modesty now would ring pretty false.

He brought them each a Scotch on the rocks and sat down beside her on the couch. "I'm glad you listened to me this morning," he said, shaking his glass and watching the ice swirl through the liquid. "I realize that you've been under a terrible strain, my dear. But I believe we'll be able to get everything straightened out in no time."

She watched his lips as he spoke, seeing rather than hearing the words. He was being Dr. Stacy now, crisply professional, soothing the troubled patient with the magic balm of his trained bedside manner. She did not understand why he chose to treat her like this now.

Surely he must know why she had come.

"All you need is a little time away from your situation." He smiled. "We doctors know very well what we're doing when we prescribe a nice long vacation. A little objectivity and distance is far more effective than a bottle of pills."

"Bill, why are you speaking to me as though I were a pimply faced adolescent?" she said with annoyance. "I didn't come here for advice. Or pills."

Lines of surprise etched around his eyes. "Oh?"

For a long moment she stared into the glass clutched tightly between her palms. Then impulsively she tilted the glass to her lips and drained it in spasmodic, almost frantic gulps. The liquid burned in her mouth, her throat.

She swallowed hard. She wanted to scream, she wanted to cry, she wanted to throw the glass in his face and walk out. What was he trying to do to her?

Why must he make her crawl?

"You know why I'm here," she whispered finally.

He shook his head slowly. "No," he said. "I'm not at all sure I do."

She felt waves of heat flooding upward toward her head, blurring her vision, dulling her thoughts. It was only the alcohol, she told herself. She had forgotten to eat again. Forgotten everything but her confusion, her fears.

She set the glass on the floor and steadied herself against the arm of the couch. "I came here to be with you," she said, her voice barely audible. Even to her own ears, the words sounded fuzzy and confused. Her stomach began to contract almost violently.

He watched her closely, yet made no move to approach her.

She wanted him to take her in his arms, to love her, to crush her with his passion. Why didn't he understand that and help her, instead of sitting there with that simpering, stupid look on his face?

Couldn't he see her need?

"I want to be with you," she almost screamed.

"Karen, I want to help you in any way I can," he said quietly. "You know that."

"Then, for God sake, make love to me."

She flung herself toward him.

He caught her and drew her close.

Her fingers tore at his clothing, tugging his shirt loose and searching beneath for the warmth of flesh.

Very gently, Bill disentangled himself and pushed her away from him. He held both of her wrists in one strong, capable hand.

"You've got to get hold of yourself," he said crisply, his tone all business now.

She threw herself forward once again, wanting him, hating him, hating herself.

"You want me," she screamed. "You know you do."

He raised his free hand and struck her a stinging blow across the cheek.

For a moment she merely stared at him, shocked and unable to comprehend. Then she began to cry, sobbing in great, heaving gasps as though she would never find peace again.

Finally the sobbing subsided, leaving her exhausted and drained.

She leaned against him limply.

He held her lightly, his long fingers moving to caress her hair, her cheek. "Tell me what's happened to you," he said, his tone tender. "Everything."

She didn't want him to know what she had been through. None of it. Yet she sensed that he desired sincerely to help her. And she knew that no doctor could cure an illness unless he knew the symptoms.

Haltingly, she told him all that had happened since the day of Steve's accident. The nervous days and endless nights. The growing tension as the demands of her body became increasingly insistent. The incident with the man in the park and her brief affair with Jean.

He listened attentively, not once interrupting the tumbling flood of words.

When she had finished, he took a pipe out of his jacket pocket, carefully filled and packed it. Inhaling flame into the bowl, he puffed reflectively for several moments.

"Well, say something," she demanded finally. "Don't just sit there and peer at me."

"There isn't really too much I can say." He leaned back against the arm of the couch and sent a cloud of smoke spiralling toward the ceiling. "As I've told you before, I feel that you require professional help of a kind I'm not qualified to give you. When you showed up tonight, I believed you had come to the same conclusion."

She shook her head vigorously. "No," she said. "I want to work this thing out by myself."

At the moment she hadn't the vaguest idea of where to begin. But all it required was courage. And time. And she felt she had enough of both to see her through this crisis.

"Karen, I want you to listen to me very carefully," Bill said. His voice and his expression encompassed a world of patience and understanding. "I am not suggesting that there is anything seriously the matter with you. I know there isn't. I simply feel that this whole situation has gotten somewhat out of hand. You can't see it clearly anymore. You've gotten so wrapped up in your own guilt and fear that you no longer realize there might be another approach."

She turned away from him and focused her attention on a black and white sketch hanging over the fireplace.

"You told me once," she said quietly, "that morality is nothing but a farce. I don't believe that, Bill. I don't think women ever do, really. They have too much to lose."

"I'm sorry now for what happened between us," he said. "For some reason I believed at the time that you would be able to see it the same way I did. As ... well, as an expedient, to help you out. I didn't believe then, as I told you, that you were really in love with Steve. I do now. You wouldn't be in this condition if you weren't."

She looked back at him now, meeting his gaze levelly for the first time. "Yes, I am," she said sincerely. "I don't suppose I knew it either. I ... I believed that ... Oh, I don't know what I believed."

"I think I do," Bill said. "On the basis of your behavior, at any rate. Somewhere you seem to have gotten the peculiar notion that sex is equivalent to love. Steve, because of the accident, was no longer capable of going to bed with you." He stroked his chin with the stem of his pipe. "I'd almost forgotten Steve's part in this," he went on after a moment. "Like most male animals, Steve believed when he lost his potency that he had automatically lost all attraction he might have for any woman."

"But, Bill, that's ridiculous," Karen insisted. "I didn't stop loving him ..."

"Of course not," Bill interrupted. "But he was afraid you would. So afraid that he became defensive, suspicious. He accused you of being unfaithful before the possibility entered your mind. And you, feeling rejected, believing he no longer desired you, decided that Steve had fallen out of love."

143

"It's all true," she admitted. The whole pattern had begun to clarify in her mind. Realistically she accepted the fact that Steve would have to work out his own problems for himself. But maybe…

"Bill, is there any hope that Steve will recover his manhood? I mean…" She stopped helplessly and peered at him closely.

Bill smiled. "I know what you mean," he said. "Of course there's hope. A man wouldn't last a month in my profession if he didn't believe there is always hope. All Steve needs is the will to recover. An incentive to go on trying. You can give him that, Karen. Only you."

She sat quiet for a long time, considering Bill's words. Remembering what Jean had said about selfishness. Karen felt that she was finally beginning to grasp the full significance of her friend's statement. Jean had tried to tell her what it means to love. To love deeply. Jean, for all her warped desires, understood more of the meaning of the word than Karen herself ever had.

For to love meant, really, to give. Uncritically, unstintingly, asking nothing in return for oneself.

Karen realized that she had never truly given to anyone without demanding an equal giving in return. Her attitude, even with Steve had been one of: I'll love you if you'll love me.

She leaned forward and rested one hand lightly on Bill's arm. "I've been such a damned fool," she said. "Such a fool. How do I say I'm sorry?"

"Well, the first thing I would suggest is that you drop that expression from your vocabulary. Once you begin functioning like a sensible human being, you won't have to be sorry for anything you do."

She flushed, but smiled. "And the second thing?"

"That you go wash your face," he said. "That mask you put on frightens me."

This time she laughed aloud. "I did it to entice you," she admitted. "I wanted to look like a kept woman."

"This may come as a terrible shock to you, Karen, but I've never found anything wrong with you exactly as you are."

His unexpected tenderness surprised her. Questioningly she peered into his face, searching for the full meaning behind his words.

He got up and walked to the fireplace. Reaching down, he knocked his pipe against the ball head of an andiron. "You know," he said casually, "when I was in med. school, I used to lie awake nights making plans for the future. I dreamed I would have the biggest and best practice in New York. And the finest apartment and the longest car. And the most beautiful wife." He paused but did not turn to look at her. "You were going to be the wife, you know."

"No," she said very quietly. "I didn't know. You never …"

"I never got around to asking you?" He turned now to face her. "That's right, I didn't. Because I hadn't quite made all the rest." He grinned. "I'm still driving a Chevvy. But we all make errors of judgment," he said. "Mine was that I forgot to take into account that you could possibly fall in love with someone else."

She rose shakily and crossed to stand in front of him. "Bill," she whispered, "I never knew. I'm so sorry."

He put his big hands on her shoulders but did not pull her to him. He looked deep into her eyes, his own bright, unhappy. "You have no reason to be," he said. "And I don't want you to be. All I want is to know that you're happy. Even if it's with another man."

She moved into his arms then, standing close, feeling his warmth and his strength against her. Yet now there was no blinding burst of passion, no crazy need to press herself against him and demand that he possess her.

There was quiet and affection and an end to pain.

CHAPTER SIXTEEN

LONG AFTER BILL had gone to sleep on the living-room couch, Karen sat in the bedroom, looking down on the morning quiet of the city. She had begun to feel as though she might never sleep again as long as she lived. Her body ached with fatigue, yet her thoughts would give her no rest.

Most of her anxieties and fears had already been dragged out into the open. Yet the biggest fear of all she had had to keep to herself. It wasn't the matter of sex that concerned her so much now. Though that was still something that would require much consideration.

It was Steve himself who worried her.

She had enough intelligence to know that the mere fact that she loved him and wanted him did not guarantee that he would want to take her back. She had already decided that she would have to tell him everything. Perhaps it would mean losing him forever. But that was a chance she would have to take. For there could never be anything worthwhile between them unless it were founded on truth. And trust.

Again and again she repeated to herself that she must be prepared to lose him. Yet she knew in her heart that she would rather die.

Bill had convinced her finally that at least a chat with his psychoanalyst friend Dr. Holden could do no one harm. She wanted to believe even now that she could work out this business for herself. But, after all, her efforts so far had been anything but successful. And at this point she could not afford to make any more mistakes.

Bill had assured her, too, that the sooner she adjusted to Steve's disability, the sooner Steve himself would be on the road to recovery. Marriage was meant to be a partnership. And it was about time she and Steve began to face up to this responsibility.

The deep, sonorous roll of a snore cut into her thoughts. She smiled.

Poor Bill. He deserved a sound sleep. He deserved all the good things of life he could get.

And Jean, too, Karen reflected. Probably lying sleepless in her bed, despising the virile husband beside her, longing for and perhaps worrying about the woman she loved.

Karen smiled ruefully, realizing suddenly that people like Jean had a far greater sexual problem than she herself could even imagine. She wondered if Jean had ever sought professional advice about her maladjustment. Perhaps, next time she saw her, she might offer the suggestion. It was about time she began helping the people who loved her.

By the time the first glow of dawn touched the house tops, Karen knew that she might just as well give up the idea of sleep altogether.

In the closet she found an old robe of Bill's and pulled it over her slip. With a huge pair of shaggy slippers, she felt warmly enough dressed and well enough covered. She had promised herself never to be carelessly dressed in front of Bill. There was no reason to make him uncomfortable.

In the kitchen she busied herself making coffee and setting out cups. For a bachelor, Bill had an immaculately clean and orderly apartment. Most likely, she thought, he had someone come in to clean. And she wondered idly if he would ever find himself another girl, someone who could appreciate him and give him the love she had denied him.

As she turned to the cupboard for silver, she heard a footstep behind her.

She whirled toward the doorway.

He sniffed appreciatively. "That coffee smells pretty good," he said. "I'm usually too lazy to make anything but instant myself."

Karen smiled. "How do you like your eggs?"

"Scrambled and plentiful. With ketchup."

He sat into the captain's chair beside the table and propped a heel on the handle of the oven door. Thoughtfully he ran his fingers through his dark, rumpled hair. "I had a couple of ideas last night that sounded pretty good in the dark," he said. "They might be of some use to you."

She broke eggs into a mixing bowl, dropping the shells into a paper bag. "What kind of ideas?"

"Well, first of all, I can't very well send Steve off to see Dr. Holden," he said. "But I feel confident that a simple man-to-man bull session might straighten him out on a couple of points."

"I hope you're right," she replied. "But I don't think he's too fond of you these days."

Bill laughed. "I don't blame him. Anybody who stabs you in the behind with a hypo a few times can become pretty obnoxious," he said. "Anyhow, I'll give it a try. This morning, while you're seeing Jim Holden. The least I can do is give him a few tips on how to keep you happy. Physically, that is."

The spoon slipped from her fingers and clattered into the sink. The vision of the last time Steve had tried to satisfy her spun across her brain. She did not want to go through that with him again. Ever.

"What is it, Karen?"

"Nothing," she lied. "It's … it's nothing. I just didn't get any sleep."

He got up and came to stand beside her. "Now, let's try that again," he said. He touched her arm. "What's the matter, Karen?"

She looked up at him, her eyes brimming with tears. "It's no use that way, Bill. For either of us. We've tried it."

He was quiet for a moment. Then he looked at her with a strange expression in his eyes. "Let me ask you a question," he said quietly. "It may sound a little foolish, but I don't think so. When you went to bed with this woman … What's her name?"

"Jean."

"Yes, Jean. When you went to bed with her, were you satisfied?"

She felt herself flushing hotly and pressed her fingertips to her cheeks. "Yes," she said softly. "Completely."

"I'm sure she didn't do anything that Steve isn't capable of doing," he said, a faint smile around his eyes. "Why were you satisfied with Jean?"

She turned away, unable to face the intensity of his gaze. "Because we … we both wanted to, I guess."

She could almost see his placid nod of satisfaction, even with her back turned toward him.

And maybe he was right. Maybe …

She spun to face him. "Oh, Bill. Do you really think …"

He smiled. "Don't you?"

Karen felt a great blossom of hope opening inside her. For the first time, she began to believe that, if Steve would only have her, they might yet achieve full happiness in their married love. Surely, she would find satisfaction. And in time, as he moved steadily toward complete recovery …

She could barely contain her excitement as Bill lingered over breakfast, bathing her in a steady flow of reassuring, cheerful words. Yet almost before she realized it, she was rushing to dress for her nine o'clock appointment with Dr. Jim Holden.

Bill let her out in front of a new, white brick apartment building. "I'll call you later on in the day," he said, "to see how everything's worked out."

For one moment Karen felt the old rush of insecurity flooding in on her. "You'd better let me call you," she said. "I'm not sure where I'll be."

"I am," he said with confidence. "Steve's got better sense than to let you go."

She watched him drive off, then turned and hurried inside.

The waiting room of Dr. Holden's office was expensively but tastefully furnished. She sat down to wait on a foam rubber sofa. Across from her, the strains of a bouncy popular tune wafted forth from an imitation fireplace.

She picked up a battered copy of *Life* magazine and riffled idly through the pages, more to use up nervous energy than to find something to read. Maybe someday she would be able to concentrate sufficiently to read. But at the moment she felt fairly ready to burst.

Every few seconds her glance darted nervously to the clock on the far wall.

Promptly at nine an enormously tall young man in baggy tweeds opened the door of the inner office. All of him looked rumpled and rather carelessly thrown together. Yet there was something infinitely comfortable about his shagginess, like the well-worn pages of a favorite volume.

"Mrs. Edgemont?" His voice was as deep and comfortable as the man himself.

She nodded nervously in reply.

"Please come in."

Somehow she managed to get to her feet and follow him inside. Her feet and her hands felt heavy and solid as bricks of ice.

He indicated the chair in front of his desk and waited for her to sit down.

"Don't we use a couch?" she blurted.

He grinned. "Not till I get to know you better," he said.

A few hours ago she would have interpreted his remark as something crudely suggestive. But now, somehow, she realized that the statement was simply banter, a light remark meant to set her at ease. How different the whole world was beginning to seem, now that she could see it clearly!

"Dr. Stacy's told me a little something about your situation," he began, settling one hip on the corner of the desk. "But I'd like to know a few other things about you before we get around to that. Let's start in the beginning." He picked up a small yellow pad and a pencil. "Where were you born?"

"Right here in New York," she said. "But I can't see what that has to do with my … my problem."

He made a notation on the pad. "Neither can I, right at the moment," he said affably. "But everyting you are and feel and think is the direct result of all that has happened to you up to this point in your life."

It seemed incredible to her that there might be a connection between the place where she was born and the fact of her disrupted marriage. Yet, as he continued to ask routine questions about her background, she found herself recalling bits and pieces of her life that must surely explain her intense insecurity and demand for emotional, and sexual, attention.

By the end of the session, Karen knew that she would return on Wednesday and many times again.

Needing a few moments to think over the experience she had just been through, Karen decided to walk the fifteen blocks to their apartment. She strolled slowly, sorting out in her mind the memory flashes she wanted to concentrate on, to understand. For only through understanding how she had become so emotionally confused could she become completely a person worthy of her husband's love.

At the thought of Steve, a smile touched her heart, her steps quickened. If he loved her, he would be patient. He would help her to regain her equilibrium and she in turn would help him. Together they would destroy this thing that had come between them. Together. Together they could do anything.

She fairly ran up the street toward home.

CHAPTER SEVENTEEN

K AREN LET HERSELF into the apartment and tiptoed down the hall toward the bedroom.

If she were to have any privacy with Steve at all, she knew, she would have to bypass the watchful Miss Proctor. The apartment lay silent and gloomy though it was already nearly eleven. She wondered if Bill had stopped by, as he had promised. And if so, why the sleeping silence?

The door to the bedroom was closed tight. Soundlessly she turned the knob and pushed gently inward.

Steve lay sprawled across the bed, one arm flung over his eyes as though to shut out the bright sunlight streaming in through the window. His head was turned slightly away from her, yet she knew he was not asleep.

"Steve," she called gently.

He gave no sign that he had heard her.

She called again. "Steve?"

Slowly he raised the arm away from his face and turned to look at her. "I can hear," he said.

She breathed a quiet sigh of relief. At least he was going to speak to her this time. She could stand almost anything better than his stubborn silences. Even his scorn, his abuse.

Tentatively she took a step closer to the bed.

"I've ... I've come home," she murmured. It sounded foolish, even to her. Yet nothing else came to her mind. All the pretty, loving speeches she had dreamed up for him had evaporated completely from her thoughts.

"What makes you think it's still home?" he said nastily. "I didn't hear anybody say it."

"Oh, Steve, please," she said, the impatience trying to creep into her tone. "Let's not fight now. I know you've been through a lot, darling." She paused, then lowered her glance. "But so have I."

"So I gather."

She looked up at him quickly. "Bill's been here?"

"Yeah. He's been here. Had a hell of a lot to say for himself, too. But I guess you know all about that."

She drew the chair up close beside the bed. "Not really. He simply told me that he wanted to have a man-to-man talk with you."

Steve snorted. "That's a laugh."

"Steve..."

"Yeah, yeah, I know. I gotta remember I'm still a man even if my wife does have to sleep all over town." He looked at her a little desperately now. "How the hell would any guy feel in my place?"

She reached out to touch his hand. He withdrew it quickly and turned away.

Taking a deep breath, Karen shut her eyes and begged for strength. Then, to change the subject for a moment, she said, "Miss Proctor must be asleep. This is the first time I've been able to sneak past her."

"She's gone," he said.

"Gone?"

"Yeah. I told Bill to take the goddamned old harpie with him. She's been drivin' me nuts, hoverin' around. I couldn't even take a crap in peace."

Karen felt some of the tension easing from her limbs. "In that case, I guess you'll be needing me," she said cheerfully.

"Guess again. He's gonna send another one. This afternoon."

Karen sighed. "All right, Steve. You've made your point."

She watched a touch of pink suffuse his pale features. "But before I go," she went on, "there are some things I have to tell you about myself."

"I don't wanta hear them."

"You're going to, whether you want to or not," she said flatly. She sat up tall in the straight-backed chair, needing all the feeling of authority she could command.

He looked as though he intended to ignore her completely. Yet Karen sensed that he was warily attentive, every fiber of his being straining toward her now, waiting, worried and a little afraid.

"First of all," she began, "despite the fact that I've been acting like a lunatic, I want you to know that I do love you. With all my heart. I've done some things I'm not proud of. At the time I honestly felt that I had no choice. But now … Well, I realize that my behavior was not that of a well-adjusted adult. I'm going to do everything I can to get myself all straightened out."

"Yeah," he muttered. "I know about that. Goddamn it, Karen. Do you think any man likes to know he's drivin' his wife nuts? I mean, you goin' to an analyst sure paints a pretty picture of me."

She sensed the deep hurt and humiliation underlying his words and she longed to put her arms around him and soothe him. But tenderness would have to wait.

"What's wrong with me has nothing to do with you, Steve. Or very little, anyhow. Most of it started way back when I was a child. You know I've always been terrified of my mother. I still am, a little."

Something close to a smile passed across his pale lips. "Who isn't?" he said. "She's enough to ruin anybody."

For once she did not bother defending the family honor. "Anyhow," she went on, "there's no reason for you to feel guilty about my emotional problems. And, since I do love you, my seeking help is certainly no threat. If anything, it could mean a tremendous improvement in our marriage."

"Huh uh," he muttered. "There's nothin' to improve. No man in his right mind puts up with a wife's being unfaithful."

"Bill told you that, too?"

"Yeah. The whole, damned, dirty picture. You sure have been havin' a ball for yourself, while all the time I'm lyin' here worryin' myself sick about you."

She had told Bill last evening that she intended to make a clean breast of everything with Steve. Still, it surprised her that Bill had taken the responsibility upon himself. If only he had warned her, had prepared her in some way for this unexpected turn.

"He tried to tell me it was all his fault," Steve went on heavily. "And I always knew he wanted your tail. But, by God, no woman really gets it unless she asks for it."

Silently, Karen sent out her thanks to Bill for his gallant move to protect her. And Jean. And probably his decision had been a wise one. It would be difficult enough for Steve to accept that she had been to bed with another man. But certainly impossible to accept that she had made love to a woman, the wife of his closest friend.

She bit back the urge to tell him the truth. Someday, in the future, when he was stronger, perhaps ...

And suddenly she realized that her future did indeed lie right here with Steve. He hadn't said or done anything yet to let her know it would be all right. Still, she knew that he was fighting her only because he felt he had to. It was a contest of wills, a proving of strengths.

And she knew she must help him prove for himself the total security of his position.

She stood up beside the bed, her hands folded, features arranged in an expression of sadness. "I guess that's everything," she said. "I suppose I'd better pack and go."

"Yeah," he said said. "I suppose you'd better."

"Yes," she echoed.

From the closet she dragged down a large, blue-checkered valise and spread it open on the floor. Without bothering to glance at him directly, she moved quickly about the room, gathering up her clothing and cosmetics and setting them into the valise.

Occasionally she glimpsed his reflection in the dressing table mirror. He had hunched himself up in bed, his eyes following her every move, lines of concern cutting deep into his forehead.

She smiled to herself and went on about the business of getting ready to leave.

Finally she tucked in the last item and dropped the lid of the valise. She felt him watching her now as she bent to snap the lock.

She stood up and began struggling with the heavy valise toward the door.

"Put that damned thing down before you hurt yourself."

Obediently she set the bag down just inside the door. She waited.

"Look, come here, will you? How the hell can I yell at you if you're way over there?"

She had never heard his voice so gentle. She felt a vast tenderness suffuse her and her heart began thumping like a pump gone wild.

He patted the bed beside him. "Right here," he said.

She sat down close, but not touching him. "What do you want to yell at me about?"

He shook his head. "Nothing," he said. "Never again." He took her hand and held it tight in his enormous paw. "That is, if you're willing to give it another try?"

"Oh, Steve, if you could only know how much I want to."

"Well, you'll get plenty of chance to show me," he said. "I promise."

She felt one eyebrow quiver into an arc. "Oh?"

"Yeah, oh," he said. He pulled her toward him and held her hard against his chest. "And if you don't believe it ..."

As his arms went around her, Karen knew that she believed him. That she always would. Her lips met his eagerly, anxiously. She was home. Home to stay.